DEATH BEHIND CLOSED DOORS

Jon Neal has a Master of Arts in Writing from Swinburne University, Australia. His poems and short stories have been published in multiple anthologies, and he was runner up in the 2010 Sydney Mardi Gras short story competition. His debut short novel *A Twin Room* was published in 2022 and reached number 1 in its Amazon category. *Death Behind Closed Doors* is the second in the Stanley Messina Investigates series. Jon lives with his partner in Sussex.

Death Behind Closed Doors

JON NEAL

Copyright © Halcyon Enterprises Ltd 2024

All rights reserved. No part of this publication may be reproduced or transmitted in any form or by any means, electronic or mechanical, including photocopy, recording, or any information storage and retrieval system, without permission in writing from the publisher

PB ISBN 9798878718417

This book is a work of fiction. Names, characters, businesses, organisations, places and events are either the product of the author's imagination or used fictitiously. Any resemblance to actual persons, living or dead, events or locales is entirely coincidental.

CHAPTER 1

Jack Sheppard elbowed his way through the crowds, cursing the sunshine. He viewed the promenade suspiciously.

The clock on the pier told him he'd arrived early.

Clifton Sands was a traditional seaside resort on the Sussex coast. The windows of the grand hotels on the seafront looked out to the English Channel, glistening today in a summer haze.

It was all a façade, he thought. That was just how his mind worked. Where others saw the innocence of children playing with buckets and spades on the beach, he saw the potential for wrongdoing. It was habit. Looking at complete strangers and musing upon the possibility of a darker side. Because from his experience, what you saw was rarely what lay beneath.

He scanned the vista again.

They'd agreed via email to meet first on neutral territory. The seafront had seemed as good a place as any. A lightness in it, he hoped, might lessen any tension. Putting the invitation in writing had given him a chance to consider his words. He knew enough of himself that he had a tendency to go at things like a bull in a china shop.

In fact, he'd rehearsed his words in his head, repeating sentences numerous times to himself. It was strange how much consideration things like this took these days. He hadn't over-thought like this in the past. There'd been a time when he'd been nimble on his feet, making decisions bravely and instinctively. But, he reminded himself, just look where that had got him.

The strains of laughter drifting up from the water's edge exacerbated a growing sense of being alone. When had it started? When had this solitary state begun? He couldn't say.

All he could be sure of was that he couldn't shake the feeling that the only way to move forward was in this imminent rendezvous, and the question of a murder.

Fifteen minutes later, Jack stood at the spot near the bandstand where they'd agreed to meet. A brass band had struck up a frantic melody and attracted curious folk to witness the spectacle of the conductor waving his baton. The sun beat down upon him. He wiped sweat anxiously from his forehead, growing concerned that they might not find each other in the throng. It had been some years since they'd seen one another. Perhaps they might not even recognise each other.

A momentary divide in the crowd provided the first glimpse of him approaching. Jack held his breath. He felt an overwhelming wave of mixed emotions of which he hadn't the words to define. Except, perhaps, for one: *relief*. Relieved to know that he was at least *here*. That was a start. That was promising.

Jack raised his hand. 'Stanley!' he called, but his voice was lost in the music and chatter. He pushed his way through the hot bodies, surprised at his sudden vigour and determination, until he reached him face to face. 'Stanley!' he said again, panting slightly.

The man before him, he was pleased to see, looked relaxed and healthy. He wore cream chinos and a dark blue polo shirt. His eyes were hidden behind a pair of sunglasses.

'I wasn't sure you'd come,' said Jack. 'I'd have understood if you hadn't. What with everything...' his words ran out of steam. He hadn't wanted to babble.

'Your email said it was important. That you need my help.'

'Yes,' said Jack. 'That's it.'

'We couldn't have chosen a busier place to meet.'

'I should've thought,' said Jack. 'I was thinking more of you. Thought perhaps you'd prefer to meet on neutral territory, so to speak.' He found himself staring at the man before him. 'You haven't changed.' It sounded sentimental the moment he said it. He'd meant it simply as an observation.

Stanley's lack of response suggested otherwise or a reluctance to discuss the past. It was always going to be the tightrope on which they'd have to tread. If there was ever to be a way forward, they would need to tiptoe carefully across the divide, trying to find the right balance.

'Shall we find a quieter place for you to explain?' asked Stanley.

'We could try one of the hotel bars? They might be cooler and less crowded than the beach.'

Stanley nodded and let Jack lead the way. The conversation faltered as they crossed the road on which a traffic jam had gnarled to a fumey halt. They made their way into one of the hotels that lined the front, remnants of heyday glamour and British seaside glory, where they came upon a wood panelled bar. Jack opted for a pint of ale whilst Stanley ordered a sparkling water.

'I was surprised to get your email,' said Stanley as they staked their claim on a table in the window. 'Of all the people, you are the last I'd think to hear from.'

'I'd heard that you'd become a private investigator. There was a story in the local newspaper about a case you'd been involved with in Littleworth. Messina is an unusual name.' It was only half of the story, of course. Too early to disclose that he'd been following Stanley's progress to ease his own conscience.

'And why would a detective require the services of a private investigator?'

Jack looked at the stained circles on the veneer surface of the table. '*Former* detective,' he said. 'I took early retirement. Aged fifty.'

He looked at Stanley directly who had removed his sunglasses. There were lines around his eyes that hadn't been there in the past. Jack wondered what background research Stanley had undertaken prior to their meeting. What private investigator wouldn't do an initial information trawl before speaking to a potential client?

'That doesn't answer the question,' said Stanley.

'No. It doesn't answer it for you. But perhaps it is connected. You see, there was a difficult case. You might say it sort of shook my confidence. It impacted upon my career.' As soon as he'd said the words, he realised how they might be misinterpreted. The tight-rope wobbled. He needed to gather his composure, and fast. 'There were mistakes made. Things got overlooked. I need a fresh pair of eyes to see what might've been done differently.'

Was there a chink of light between them?

Jack ran out of words. Men like him didn't express emotions. He only hoped he'd said enough.

He waited. Stanley had turned his head and appeared to be thinking. He was looking at the distant horizon.

Eventually he returned Jack's gaze.

'Tell me more…' he said.

Jack took a breath. He felt his shoulders relax. It would be safer on the familiar grounds of outlining a case. His years of experience had equipped him with a solid understanding of the stages of an investigation. He recalled past relish at standing before a team, confidently ensuring that procedure was followed and that everyone had an opportunity to contribute. The authoritative voice he'd had back then unexpectedly returned as he began to convey the facts:

'On Saturday the twenty seventh of August last year, the body of a young woman was discovered in the garden of a house here in Clifton Sands. It was the busy August bank holiday weekend. Her name was Ashleigh James.' Jack looked to Stanley who gave a nod. 'You know of the case?'

'I remember it being reported in the news at the time,' said Stanley.

Jack recalled his constant professional battle with the media. It had always been a fractious relationship. He'd always needed journalists to report appeals for information or potential witnesses, but frequently got frustrated at their hunger for morbid details. 'The murder of a pretty young thing was bound to attract attention.'

Stanley flinched.

It was his language, he supposed. On reflection, *pretty young thing* didn't sound too good. Those were just the type of words they'd used. A sort of verbal shorthand to express things quickly. It was odd how different they sounded beyond the confines of the force.

He sought to clarify: 'I mean, the media always jumps on the tragedy of an attractive young woman being murdered. Much more shocking, I guess.'

Stanley remained impassive. He looked thoughtful. 'You'll have to remind me of the details. You say she was murdered? How?'

'A single blow to the head. Her body was discovered in a summerhouse of the garden of a house where she was employed as a nanny.' Jack nodded towards the western end of town. He didn't know how much Stanley knew of the local geography, but hopefully there'd be time to explore everything in more detail together.

Jack recalled arriving at the crime scene in his official capacity and seeing her lying lifeless upon the wooden floor. Her skin had the quality of alabaster. She wasn't the first dead body he'd seen. All just in a day's work.

'The crime scene was secured immediately so that protocol could be followed.'

'By which you mean forensics? Evidence gathering?'

'Yes,' said Jack firmly, sounding perhaps a little defensive. It was one of the areas that had come under scrutiny in the following difficult months when questions had started to be asked about the effectiveness of the investigating team. And, inevitably, the person at their helm.

The strange sensation of a lump forming in his throat caught him by surprise. He didn't want to admit it, but that shadow had hung over him before then.

'Are you okay?' asked Stanley.

Jack swallowed. His eyes had grown unnervingly misty. He hoped that Stanley hadn't noticed. He reached out to take a sip of his ale.

Stanley spoke quietly: 'You said it shook your confidence?'

Had he said that? It shook him to think that he'd shared that so soon. To share something so personal that he hadn't dared share with anyone else. Perhaps, he wondered, he'd been subconsciously offering a part of himself in the hope of rebuilding his trust or maybe having the openness reciprocated. Although, from what he'd observed so far, Stanley's walls looked to be built high and strong.

'Somewhere along the line,' said Jack, 'it was like I'd had a tiny little chip in the windscreen. So small that you could barely see it with the naked eye. But bit by bit it began to spread out across the glass. Until, one day, it had compromised the entire screen. And in turn, the unwavering belief I'd held in the police force and my position within it faltered.'

'The person who murdered Ashleigh James was never found?'

'No,' said Jack.

'Then let me ask you frankly,' said Stanley, 'are you asking me to assist you solve a cold case murder? Or are you hoping I can help you salvage your reputation as a detective?'

Jack hung his head. He wasn't used to being the one on the end of questions. That was usually his role. He opted to lob one back in response: 'Do they have to be mutually exclusive?'

'I just don't want there to be any misunderstandings between us.'

'So you'll help? You'll review the case with me?' For the first time in months, the days ahead held some sense of promise. The possibility of purpose filled him with optimism.

'We'll need to discuss my fee.'

Jack waved the comment away dismissively. No amount would be too high for this opportunity. 'Minor details,' he said.

It would be an opportunity for redemption, in so many ways.

He offered up his hand above the table and their half empty glasses. For an instant, he wondered whether Stanley would respond, until gently he extended his arm and grasped his fingers round his own. Too soon, perhaps, to define what the gesture represented. Only that it heralded a possible new beginning. A fresh start.

He pulled his hand away self-consciously.

Why had he contacted Stanley Messina? Why *had* he?

CHAPTER 2

They agreed for Jack to pick Stanley up the next morning and travel the short journey across town together. If there had been any surprise at Stanley's current address, Jack hadn't shown it.

From the passenger seat, Stanley watched the passing scenes of a Sunday morning. On a playing field parents huddled on side lines watching their children kick a football about. The pavements were dotted with dog walkers being pulled along by leads.

Only now did he wonder whether Jack insisting on being behind the wheel might have more to do with him being in charge. He was probably over-thinking it.

'You say she'd always lived in Clifton Sands?' said Stanley. The correct term was victim, which sounded cool and clinical, so he chose not to use it.

'That's right. Clifton Sands born and bred.'

The car drew to a halt at a set of traffic lights. Stanley looked at the plume rising from the car in front.

'Seaside towns are interesting places, don't you think?' he said. 'Behind the postcard images selling the escapism, they're often just like everywhere else. Another town of people just trying to make a go of it.'

'You could argue that things are tougher. Unemployment is traditionally higher, as are the rates of crime and substance abuse.'

Stanley wondered why that was.

The lights turned green and they moved forward again.

'I don't feel I've had an opportunity to brief you on all the details,' said Jack. 'It seems a bit unconventional.'

Their initial meeting hadn't covered details of the case or how the pair of them might work together. It occurred to Stanley that their approaches would be different. Hadn't that been the point of Jack approaching him?

'I think it's better that way,' said Stanley. 'It gives me an opportunity to put things together in a way that makes sense to me, without prejudice. I'm bound to ask questions as we move forward.'

'Of which I'll be happy to answer them. And when you're good and ready I'll introduce you to the case files.'

'You still have access to them? Despite leaving the force?'

'I took a copy of everything.'

Stanley wasn't sure of the ethics. A little niggle dug at him. Hadn't questionable choices been the reason their paths had met back then? His thoughts pulled in multiple directions. He must pull the shutters down in his brain. He'd agreed to review the case of a murdered young woman. The rest of it would have to be compartmentalised and locked away.

They were entering into an estate of nineteen seventies housing which held none of the sparkle of Clifton Sands's beaches. It slumbered still on this weekend morning.

'Here we are,' said Jack as he pulled up in front of a terrace of houses. 'Number forty-seven Primrose Drive.'

The grimy double-glazing, unkempt gardens and peeling wood cladding looked at odds with the pretty street name.

'How do you want to play this?' asked Jack as he unclipped his seatbelt. 'I'm happy to take the lead. Not sure it's necessary to play good cop bad cop on this one.'

Stanley nodded, hoping that his agreement wouldn't be seen as a willingness to be subservient. He might not have chosen to drive, but there would be no hierarchy as far as he was concerned. 'Let's just play it by ear,' he said. 'See how we go.'

On the front door opening, Jack introduced Stanley and Reece James to one another. Jack had already been in contact, so

Reece had been expecting them.

The inside of the house was stuffy and airless. Stanley's nostrils twitched. It smelt of damp washing that hadn't had an opportunity to air.

Reece wore faded jeans and a T-shirt emblazoned with a logo that Stanley didn't recognise. Maybe a reference to a cult film or TV show. He wore wooden beaded bangles on one wrist. They were the trappings of someone clinging to their youth or refusing to follow the crowd. His hair, however, whilst cropped short betrayed his age having turned a metallic looking salt and pepper.

'Come in,' said Reece, ushering them through to a cluttered lounge. Stanley always took note of first impressions. And yet, in this instance, he felt that he was being equally sized up as Reece's sharp eyes focused on him with laser-like concentration.

'Good of you to see us on a Sunday morning,' said Jack.

'It's actually convenient,' Reece replied, sweeping up into his arms a mess of magazines and newspapers scattered on a cracked vinyl sofa. Stanley saw cryptic crosswords completed with jagged handwriting. 'It's not worth my time opening the shop on a Sunday morning. No passing trade. Sometimes in winter I don't even bother opening at all. Please, take a seat...'

Stanley sensed Jack bristle as they sagged together on sitting down. It was, perhaps. the closest they'd ever been.

Reece looked momentarily surprised at the items in his arms and glanced unsuccessfully for a clear surface to dump them. With a little shrug he placed them on the carpet where, Stanley suspected, they would remain long after their departure. He moved in quick little jolts though whether this was his natural demeanour or out of anxiety, Stanley couldn't be sure. Eventually, he sat down on a retro swivel chair.

Stanley anticipated a gentle transition into the conversation from Jack. A thoughtful, 'How have things been?' or 'How are you keeping?' But it wasn't to be.

'So as you know,' Jack launched in, 'the investigation into

Ashleigh's murder was wound down. The powers that be felt that they couldn't justify the ongoing resources to support the case. It was never, of course, officially closed. It just sort of remains in limbo.'

'In limbo,' Reece echoed. 'Yes, in limbo.'

'As I said to you on the phone, I've now retired from the force but would like to review the case in my own time with a third party. Just to make sure that every possible avenue was identified and followed up.'

'I wondered whether you had some new information. Hoping that something might've come to light.'

'I'm afraid not. There are no new leads.'

Stanley hoped that the man's expectations weren't being raised unrealistically. 'We'll do everything we can to re-examine every aspect of the case,' he said. 'But there are no guarantees that the outcome will be any different from the current one.'

'At the very least,' said Reece, 'it'll make me feel as if *something* is being done. Rather than being in this constant state of helplessness. Feeling like we've let her down. Although I doubt the Rainsfords are affected by it now.'

Jack half turned his head in Stanley's direction. 'Ashleigh was employed as a nanny by Oliver and Jacinta Rainsford. They have a young daughter, Sophie.'

'It was just a mere inconvenience to them,' said Reece. 'Nothing more than a passing irritation. From what I understand, life continues pretty nicely for them now. With a new nanny in place, they carry on just as before.' His knee was fidgeting. 'You have to worry for her though, eh? After what Ashleigh experienced.'

Jack nodded as if he understood. Stanley would need to be filled in on all these finer details. There were many blanks in the current picture he was building.

Reece looked almost imploringly at them both. 'I wish sometimes that someone could tell me that it wasn't all my fault. I mean, when she said that she was going to be a 'live-in' nanny, I wonder whether I should've tried to persuade her otherwise…'

'But you weren't to know that she'd come to harm,' said Jack.

'No,' said Reece. 'I'm not sure about her decision making at that time. Can't be sure that it wasn't just a knee-jerk reaction. A spur of the moment thing. It wasn't an easy time for any of us.'

Again, Stanley didn't feel over all the salient details.

'Family life isn't always straightforward,' said Jack.

Stanley realised that he knew nothing of Jack's life despite his own having been laid bare. It wasn't a level playing field.

'How long had Ashleigh lived with and worked for the Rainsfords?' asked Stanley.

'About three months, if I remember correctly,' said Jack.

'Yes, that's right,' Reece confirmed. 'Up until then she'd still been here. Just the two of us. I keep meaning to do something about her bedroom. I mean, clear it out, redecorate. But I can't find the strength to tackle it. In all honesty, I still can't bring myself to look in there…'

'Would you mind if we looked?' asked Stanley. 'It might help me to get to know Ashleigh a little more. Who she was as a person.'

'Please, feel free,' said Reece.

Placing his hand upon the door handle, Stanley suddenly felt as if they were intruding. As if he was about to disturb ghosts.

He paused.

'Everything ok?' asked Jack who stood imposingly beside him.

'There's a lot for me to catch up on, that's all. Lots of gaps in the story.'

Stanley pushed on the handle and the door gave way silently on its hinges. The pale purple curtains were half-drawn giving the room a reverential mood. It felt like looking at photograph. A space captured in time.

There was a sweet dusty smell.

'A bit morbid,' Jack said quietly so that Reece downstairs would not hear. 'I mean, shutting her room up like this. Treating it like some kind of mausoleum.'

It didn't strike Stanley as unusual. Entirely understandable not to want to face the painful truth, being stuck in that moment of trauma.

The room was furnished sparsely. A nod perhaps towards Ashleigh not having lived here for a period of time before her death. Stanley wondered how many belongings she had been able to take to her place of employment. The ins and outs of working as a nanny weren't familiar to him.

There was a single bed with a mauve duvet on it. A shabby wooden desk, probably once used for completing school homework, now looked to have been used latterly as a dressing table with a mirror on the wall above it. Stanley saw that a hairbrush remained on its surface. Threads of black hair were still tangled in it.

'Ashleigh lived here alone with her father?'

'Step-father,' Jack said. 'Reece wasn't her biological father.'

Stanley opened a door to a small wardrobe to see a mixture of garments hanging within. He noticed a pair of childish pink slippers beside a pair of high heels. They condensed a sense of the entire room, of being a mix of both child and adult. Ashleigh, he thought, was of that age where she was transitioning from adolescence to adulthood. Not always an easy time.

'How old did you say she was?' asked Stanley.

'Nineteen.'

'What about her mother?'

'A sad story there, I recall. She died of a rare degenerative condition. From what I understand, Ashleigh had looked after her for some time. Teenager carer, I think they call it. Helen James died not six months before Ashleigh.'

Stanley thought of the man downstairs and the grief that he must have endured. Two losses within such a short space of time.

'And Ashleigh's natural father?'

'He was killed in a motorbike accident when Ashleigh was eight. It was a few years later that Helen met Reece and they became a family.'

Around the mirror of the dressing table, Stanley peered at a smattering of photos stuck to the wall. In a world where digital images on phones and devices were the norm, he reasoned that to have taken the time to print these pictures must demonstrate some personal importance or significance.

The dark hairs from the hairbrush matched the shade of both a girl and the young woman she was to become in many of the shots. Selfies with others in various locations. Frozen scenes of life being lived.

'Not much here for you to go on,' said Jack. 'And everything's itemised in the case files. Just thought it might give you a bit of context.'

Stanley scanned the room again. A teddy bear sat alone on her abandoned pillow.

'I have a lot of questions,' said Stanley.

He noticed something of a brief smile on Jack's lips. 'Now, why am I not surprised to hear that…'

CHAPTER 3

The Rainsford's house was situated on a wide tree-lined avenue. From where Jack had parked, Stanley could see its impressive double frontage with a heavy wooden door at its centre. A white Porsche was pulled up on the sweeping driveway.

Following their visit to Reece James yesterday, Stanley had mulled over what he'd learnt so far. As he unclipped his seatbelt, he was struck by the contrast between the two houses. They seemed to represent two very different sides to Clifton Sands.

'There's some serious money here,' said Jack. Stanley wasn't sure whether there was a hint of envy in his tone. 'How the other half live, eh?'

'I don't suppose employing a nanny comes cheap,' Stanley said, keeping his mind focused on the investigation.

Getting out of the car, Stanley took in the streetscape. The area looked to be quiet. There was no passing traffic. No reason to visit this road unless you lived here or had business to attend to.

A squirrel bounded up one of the vast trees. Its lively presence felt at odds with the shadow of a murder.

'Just a heads up,' said Jack, 'but Jacinta Rainsford can be a bit prickly.'

Stanley didn't answer. He'd prefer to make his own judgements.

As they stepped close to the immense front door, surrounded by carved stone, Stanley noticed a CCTV camera positioned above the mantle.

'That wasn't there in the past,' said Jack. 'More security conscious these days, I'd say.'

Stanley let Jack rap on the black cast-iron knocker.

The woman who opened the door was dressed in casual sportswear and clutched a small white towel. 'Detective inspector Sheppard,' she said. 'And you must be Stanley Messina.'

Stanley nodded.

'I won't shake your hand,' she said. 'I'm sweaty. I've being doing Pilates.'

Her blonde hair was scraped back into a tight ponytail, and despite having been exercising, still looked to be made-up immaculately. Stanley noticed her painted talons.

'Thank you for your time,' said Jack.

As they crossed the threshold, Stanley placed her age as in her early thirties.

The entrance hall was of no lesser scale than the house's exterior, with a wooden staircase that twisted half way up its height leading to the floor above. A modern silver and glass chandelier hung above the space.

'I'm between flights,' she said, pushing the door closed behind them, separating the world beyond from the apparent luxury within. She looked at Stanley. 'I work for an airline. Long-haul routes. A string of days on, a string of days off. Not exactly nine to five.'

Stanley doubted that such an occupation could've afforded such a property. 'Must play havoc with your body-clock,' he said.

'One of the downsides, yes. But you sort of get used to living with constant jet-lag. And besides, the perks outweigh any of those types of things.'

She led them through to an expansive kitchen diner. The units and island were furnished in a contemporary yet classic style. Somebody here had an eye for design and the finer things in life. The space was full of natural light because of a wall of bi-fold glazed doors that had been pulled back to create a seamless flow out on to a patio which led to a series of rising landscaped terraces.

'I can't offer you anything you haven't already heard before,' she said, briskly. 'I'm not keen to re-visit it all again, to be honest. Can't say it felt too good being interrogated. Being treated like a suspect.'

Like? Stanley wondered. Jacinta's words held scant sympathy for the murdered young woman. Only, it sounded, for the way in which she had been treated because of it.

'We have the statement you made at the time. That's all we need right now,' said Jack. 'It's just for Stanley to review the evidence thoroughly, he needs to look at the crime scene in person. Not just from a description.'

She turned from Jack to Stanley. 'Perhaps you'll appreciate more than your colleague that this *'crime scene'* happens to be a home. I don't think DI Sheppard always understood that.'

'I…' Jack started.

'There was nothing *human* about how the investigation was undertaken. It felt to us like you trampled on everything.'

'A young woman, who was employed by you and your husband, was found murdered in your garden. Of course the focus was to be on her, rather than making sure that any of your garden beds didn't get trodden on.'

Jack's tone was defensive.

The exchange brought back to Stanley in a flash his own experiences. He mentally swatted it away immediately and sought to bring down the tension in the room. 'It must've been a very difficult time. And I'm sorry that any re-visiting of the case might bring back memories and feelings. But I want to reassure you that I'll be as sensitive as I can.'

'Thank you,' she said to Stanley, inferring in her voice that this thanks didn't extend to Jack. 'We want an answer to what happened to Ashleigh as much as anyone. It didn't always feel that the police understood that. They treated us *all* as if we'd killed her. We were made to feel guilty for even *employing* a nanny.'

Jack looked moody. He shoved his hands in his trouser pockets.

Stanley continued: 'I'll be looking at whether there were shortcomings in the investigation. Trying to see things from all angles.'

This appeared to appease her a little. 'It's Sophie I'm concerned for, you understand. She's only four.'

'Your daughter?'

'Yes. She's had so much disruption in the last year. I worry about the impact it's had on her. Worried that it might've done some kind of long-lasting damage. You hear of such things, don't you?'

'Is she here now?' asked Stanley, softly.

'No. Bernadette's taken her to the park. You'll want to talk to her too, I suppose. Bernadette, I mean.'

'Bernadette Greene replaced Ashleigh as Sophie's nanny,' Jack explained.

Again, Stanley felt inadequately prepared. He wished he'd had an opportunity to familiarise himself with at least the broad details of the case. In doing so, he might've known what questions to ask. Instead, it felt as if he was taking stabs in the dark. No different, he thought, to what Jack must have felt at the beginning of the case.

It was clear that Jacinta was not about to offer any hospitality. No tea or coffees were going to be made. And Stanley guessed that her slim waist meant that no biscuits were in the house.

'As I said,' Jacinta continued, 'Sophie's faced a lot of disruption. We *all* have. Oliver and I are, of course, more than happy to support you in your review. We just ask that it's done discreetly.'

'Is Oliver around?' asked Jack.

'No,' she said. 'He's up in London at the office. Will be staying up there for most of the week.'

'We'd like to catch up with him at some point too.'

'I told him that would be likely. He would've been here this morning, but the business is incredibly busy. It always is at this time of year.'

Stanley was mentally writing a list of questions in his head. Things that he wanted clarification on. But for now, it felt right simply to observe and listen. To ask anything too obvious might give an impression of not being sharp.

'If you've seen the case files,' said Jacinta to Stanley, 'you'll know that I was the one who found her.'

Stanley hadn't known this but nodded anyhow. 'In the garden.'

'Yes,' she said. 'Well, in the summerhouse to be specific.'

'Can you tell me a little about it?' asked Stanley.

She leant against the kitchen island and folded her arms. It was the look of a person who had described the situation many a time.

'It was a rare Saturday when we could be together as a family and it coincided with one of Ashleigh's rostered days off. Oliver and I thought it would be nice to spend a day with Sophie at the beach.'

'Did Ashleigh have any plans herself?' asked Stanley.

'She didn't say so. There had been a boy on the scene, but as far as we could make out it had all been a bit on and off.'

'Lorenzo Conti?' asked Jack.

'Yes,' said Jacinta. 'Oliver didn't like the idea of Ashleigh having a boy at the house. But as far as I know, that day Ashleigh was going to spend the day alone. She said that she enjoyed her own company.'

Stanley wanted to ask more about the boy she'd mentioned, but thought that interrupting her might disrupt her flowing train of thought.

'We spent the day at the beach as planned. It was later that afternoon that we came back to find the house empty. And yet, the bi-fold doors here hadn't been closed. To begin with, we wondered whether Ashleigh had just popped out somewhere. But it would've been very unlike her not to have locked everything up. She was always very good at that type of thing.

'I looked out to the garden initially, but didn't see anything unusual. It was only a little later that I began to feel concerned. I don't know why. I just remember looking round the house more closely for any signs as to where she'd gone. And eventually, I wandered up the garden.'

The three of them looked in the direction of the terraces. Higher up, near the rear of the garden, stood a wooden summerhouse.

'It hadn't drawn my attention,' she said, 'because her body was inside, out of sight. The door to the summerhouse was closed.'

The list of questions in Stanley's head grew ever longer.

It was helpful to hear the description first-hand, and to see the crime scene in person.

'Had you noticed anything different in Ashleigh's behaviour prior to that day?' asked Stanley.

'No,' she said. 'I can't say that I had.'

Stanley wondered whether Jacinta was the type to notice much in the behaviour of others. Particularly staff. It was something to consider.

'Would you mind if I looked at the summerhouse?' asked Stanley.

'No,' she said. 'Not at all.'

She remained in the house whilst Stanley and Jack climbed the steps.

'I told you she'd be prickly,' Jack muttered under his breath. 'She was like that from the first moment I met her.'

Stanley thought it best not to say what immediately sprung to mind. Instead, he turned his attention to scrutinising the surroundings.

'Can this garden be accessed from the rear?' he asked.

'Yes. There's a gate concealed at the far end.'

'And where does that go?'

'It has direct access to the downs. It's near the foot of the country park.'

Stanley knew that the south downs stretched along the south coast for many miles. It was a picturesque destination popular with tourists.

'So anyone could've entered the property that afternoon?'

'You're wondering whether it was a stranger. Well, it's not impossible, but the weight of evidence points towards the perpetrator being someone known to Ashleigh. The postmortem showed no signs of interference with the body.'

'So it wasn't sexually motivated.'

'And the apparent lack of struggle from her suggests that person who killed her wasn't a stranger.'

They reached the summerhouse. Through the grimy windows, the interior hung with cobwebs. Unsurprising that it looked not to be used now. Others might've been quick to tear it down. To remove the reminder of what had happened there.

'And the forensics?' asked Stanley.

'Nothing of significant interest. There was nothing here that couldn't be explained away.'

He looked again at the structure. A quiet place to think alone, perhaps. An intimate place to meet with someone. Maybe even a place to hide.

A child's voice rang out.

From where they stood, the interior of the house looked like the stage in a theatre. And on its boards stood three females of different ages acting out their various roles. Mother, daughter and nanny. Their initial interaction looked to evolve into a whispered explanation, which resulted in faces turning towards them. Just a little too far away to label their expressions.

'Seen enough?' asked Jack.

Stanley glanced at the closed door of the summerhouse. He thought of Ashleigh lying lifeless within. What chance was there of him finding an answer when so many had failed? The weeds around them looked thick and gnarly.

'Let's move on,' he said.

CHAPTER 4

With Jacinta's insistence that Sophie be protected from further investigations still at the forefront of his mind, Jack waited until the young girl had been ushered from view before saying, 'I think the coast is clear now.'

Stanley held back and let him lead the way back down to the house.

Ashleigh's successor, Bernadette Greene, stood waiting for them in the kitchen. She smiled affectionately at him. 'I remember you,' she said. 'You asked me questions about Ashleigh.'

'That's right,' said Jack. She didn't look to have visibly changed. She was petite in stature, almost like a doll. Jack wondered whether her large black eyelashes were false. He didn't really know about such things. 'And this is Stanley Messina. He's a private investigator.'

'I'm helping to look back over the investigation,' Stanley explained. 'To see whether there were any things that might be worth exploring again.'

'That's what Jacinta told me. She said you'd probably like to see Ashleigh's room.'

'Which is your room now?' asked Stanley.

'Yes,' said Bernadette. 'Come, I'll show you.'

She almost tip-toed across the hallway, then daintily pranced fawn-like up the grand staircase. At its summit, she led them along a landing laid with plush cream carpet to what was her bedroom at the rear of the house overlooking the garden and the sloping downs beyond.

Bernadette stood aside and let them look around. She

appeared tiny in the space.

The room, unsurprisingly, retained nothing of its previous occupant. Jack wondered whether it was a pointless exercise. There was not much to see at all. With its white walls and bedding, the bedroom's stark appearance was impersonal. Only a cork noticeboard on a wall had attracted Stanley's attention.

Amongst a display of what looked to be a proud collection of various certificates were pinned photographs reminiscent of those in Ashleigh's former bedroom at Primrose Drive.

'I miss her every day,' said Bernadette. 'She was my best friend.'

'You knew her for a long time?' asked Stanley.

'Oh yes,' said Bernadette. 'We became friends at primary school. Then we moved up to the same secondary school. And eventually we studied childcare together. She was more like a sister to me. I spent a lot of time at her house when we were growing up. I still try to keep in contact with her dad, but I…'

'Go on?' said Jack.

'…but I worry sometimes that seeing me only reminds him of not having Ashleigh anymore. He's never said that to me, to be fair. He usually just frets about me being here, in this house. As if he can't separate the two of us in his mind.'

'So you don't think his concerns are valid?' Stanley asked.

'Oliver and Jacinta have made the house more secure since last summer. There are cameras everywhere now. And the gate at the back of the garden has a padlock on it.'

Jack wasn't sure whether she'd misunderstood the question, or if she truly held no concerns at living where her best friend had been murdered.

As if she had read his mind, she added: 'I know it looks weird. Me living here, doing the job that Ashleigh did. But we were so close. By being here, I feel that we're still together. I spent a lot of time with Sophie, so I like to think that it helps her too. Something familiar. A bit of continuity.'

Stanley looked to be deep in thought. 'What, would you say,

was Ashleigh's working relationship with Oliver and Jacinta like?'

'I'd say it was a bit strained at times,' she replied.

'What makes you say that?'

'They hadn't had a nanny before. It was new to them, and Ashleigh. She'd only ever worked in a nursery before. I think there were probably some tussles about where the boundaries lay over her responsibilities. And then there was the ongoing debate about Lorenzo...'

'Her boyfriend.'

'Yes. Ashleigh felt that they only saw the worst in him. Thought that he was from the wrong side of the tracks. She was never shy about standing up for what she believed in. She was strong. That's what I miss. Her *strength*. She was loyal to those she cared for. She was the fiercest protector you could ever ask for.'

Her words brought back to Jack the discernible currents of friction that had run through the case. They had run in many directions. Differences of opinion that had seemed to link those close to Ashleigh like threads on a spider's web. Petty conflicts to be pursued which had ultimately resulted in nothing.

That friction had come to mar not only Ashleigh's recent history. In Jack's opinions, they'd also spilled over into his own career.

'Do you have anything to do with Lorenzo now?' he asked, sounding abrupt.

She paused to consider her answer. 'I don't have a lot of spare time to socialise,' she said. Jack supposed that her prior description of the Rainsford's opinion of Ashleigh's boyfriend might make her reluctant to disclose any ongoing communication.

Jack thought she looked fragile. He wondered whether she was vulnerable. 'It's been a year now. Is there anything that's occurred to you since then? Has anything crossed your mind about the situation since living and working here? Any insights that might help me?'

It was too many questions. Always, he thought, guilty of asking too many questions.

'There's just one thing,' she said. 'It goes round and round in my head. Over and over again…'

'Yes?' Jack said hopefully.

'Why didn't you find who did it? Why didn't you find her killer?'

He noticed that she had scrunched her hands up anxiously at her sides. An unspoken concern, perhaps, of the sort that Ashleigh's father had expressed for her.

Jack floundered for the right words. There was no simple answer.

Before he had an opportunity to form his thoughts, Stanley spoke: 'That's what we hope to find out. But, in the meantime, if anything else should occur to you, however small or silly it might seem, we ask that you contact us…' And with that, he withdrew a contact card from his wallet and passed it to her.

At the foot of the stairs, a young girl interrupted their passage, bounding energetically into the hallway. Her pigtails bobbed as she glanced back to the room from which she'd escaped her mother's clutches.

'Hello,' she said confidently, almost precociously. It was her own environment, Jack thought. No surprise that she'd be comfortable within it. 'I'm Sophie.'

Bernadette rounded on the young girl and seized her tiny hand. 'These are my friends,' she said. 'Jack and Stanley. They came to visit me.'

Jack sensed Jacinta's shadow approaching. Her express wishes that Sophie should be distanced from them rang sharply in his ears. He hoped that this unplanned convergence wouldn't scupper their agreement.

From Sophie's lowly position, she eyeballed Jack. She looked inquisitively at his immense height.

'Do you like to play games?' she asked.

'I like football,' he replied. 'Is that what you mean?'

She nodded. 'I like playing football too. Don't I, Bernadette?'

'Yes,' said Bernadette.

Jacinta appeared at the doorway. She looked to be judging how the interaction was unfolding. Her assertive stance had the air of a mother hen. Or more likely, Jack thought, a maternal wolf. Her silence warned them to be wary of their words.

'My favourite game used to be skipping,' said Sophie. 'I would skip all the time. Skip. Skip. Skip. I'd skip everywhere. Do you like to skip?'

Jack felt Stanley watching him out of the corner of his eye. The collar of his shirt felt tight and hot. 'I don't do a lot of skipping, no.'

'Me neither these days. Grown out of it.'

Jacinta moved into the hallway. 'We don't want to hold these gentlemen up,' she said. 'I expect they've got places they need to be…'

Sophie's attention remained undeterred by her mother's attempted intervention. If anything, she looked to hold Bernadette's hand tighter and sidle closer into her side. She swung her face up to her companion. 'We should play football with him one day. We should, shouldn't we?'

Bernadette didn't raise her hopes. 'We need to let them get on their way…' She ushered Sophie reluctantly in the direction of the kitchen. 'Let's see what we can make for lunch…'

'Then can you tell me a story? You're better than mummy at that. You do all the voices and everything…' The girl twisted her head, stumbling over her own steps. 'Goodbye then,' she said directly to Jack. 'Goodbyyyye…'

Jack struggled to find something appeasing to say to Jacinta who he noticed was already opening the front door to signal their departure. They had used up their allotted time. Overstayed, perhaps, their welcome.

And as the latch clicked firmly shut behind them, Jack looked at Stanley and gave a shrug.

*

After a quick drive into the town centre, Jack sat facing Stanley across a table in one of Clifton Sands's numerous coffee shops.

'Espresso?' he remarked, pouring two sachets of sugar into his own frothy cappuccino.

'Keeps the mind sharp,' said Stanley.

'Perhaps I ought to consider it. Might cut down on the calories too,' he said, dunking a spoon into his cup and stirring.

'Not doing enough skipping these days, eh?' Stanley jibed.

'Watch it.'

The smirk on Stanley's face made Jack feel more at ease. It softened a niggling concern that Stanley's exterior would ultimately prove to be impenetrable. A hard egg to crack, perhaps. So far, Stanley had kept his thoughts frustratingly to himself.

Out of habit, Jack scanned the room. It was the curse of having worked in the police force for too long. Knowing too much about too many people. Having crossed too many paths. Experience had taught him that people did things bad things in life. People had the capacity to do wicked things. Some, he knew, were truly evil.

'Looking for something?' said Stanley.

'Force of habit. Always on the lookout. Any signs of trouble.'

Stanley shook his head.

Jack fought an urge to tackle some of the things that remained unspoken between them. Be patient, he told himself. It's too soon to go wading into the choppy waters.

Instead, he kept to the safe ground of the case at hand.

'What did you make of the set up at the Rainsford's gaff? Not your average home, right?'

Stanley straightened his espresso cup. 'It's too early for me to say. I want to gather the facts so that I can look at things objectively.'

'You think my opinions have clouded my judgement,' said Jack.

'I don't think anything, yet. People live different lives. That doesn't mean that one is necessarily better than another. Just different.'

Jack hoped it wasn't going to become a lecture. He could do without the sanctimonious act. If it hadn't been for his wariness of their history, he would've said so. He slurped noisily from his cup before plonking back on its saucer.

Stanley smirked again.

'Something amusing? Do you think I'm guilty of making assumptions about people?'

'I think you're guilty of having a milk moustache,' said Stanley.

Jack felt his face redden. He wiped the froth swiftly from above his upper lip.

He'd missed this. The moments of companionable time with colleagues. Those times that they'd shared bellyaching laughter at their banter, or the adrenalin buzz of achieving a breakthrough or chasing down a guilty party. A blur of days, lived unappreciatively, shining bright in his memory.

'You're not comfortable with this way of working,' said Stanley.

Jack thought of the mapped out sprawl on whiteboards and the copious digital data used to track a case.

'Guess I've just got to trust that we're working toward the same objective. Two sides of the same coin. No one way better or worse. Just different.'

Jack's smugness at handing Stanley's words back to him, soon deflated at the failure to gain a reaction. Infuriating, to say the least.

CHAPTER 5

The following day, Stanley drove to the address Jack had scribbled on the back of a receipt in confident looped handwriting. He felt better being back behind the wheel of his own car.

Stanley hadn't been sure of responding to Jack Sheppard's initial email. Just seeing Jack's name in his inbox had shot an icy chill down his spine. He'd thought about deleting it, afraid that opening it might risk events turning sour again. Just when things seemed to be improving.

Things *were* getting better, weren't they?

Tentatively, his budding career as a private investigator was beginning to grow. That, surely, must count for something.

And yet, he still wrestled with memories of who he used to be, with thoughts flashing back when he least expected them. They burst into the present like a rampaging uninvited guest, confronting him with that prior version of himself. A man who had never doubted wearing his heart on his sleeve.

A stream of cars headed away from the town centre.

He didn't want to be cynical. Although it was a challenge not to be. Hard not to baulk at how naïve he'd been.

The car interior suddenly felt very large and empty. It was a sensation he'd been experiencing on a growing basis. A jolting reminder of how independent he'd become.

It was, unexpectedly, spending time with Jack that had prompted him to remember the jovial, sociable ghost of himself. A person that he could hardly reconcile with his current self.

Stanley fixed his eyes on the road ahead. The past lingered in his peripheral vision. If, as he'd trained himself to do, he could re-focus his attention on his work, the chances of tripping over himself would diminish. It was a constant struggle.

The irony of now being employed by former DI Sheppard wasn't lost on Stanley.

He clutched the steering wheel as he navigated his way through a series of roads with grass verges and ornamental cherry trees. The houses were dwarfed by the steep green slopes of the downs beyond.

He wondered whether he'd made a wrong turn. The genteel air of suburbia looked to be at odds with Stanley's opinion of Jack. It felt too polite. Too soft.

Number eighty-six was one of the many semi-detached bungalows. Stanley pulled the car up close to the grass verge and peered at the mock leadlight windows beyond the rose bushes in the front garden. Jack's beast of a car was backed on to a driveway behind a pair of dainty wrought iron gates. It looked out of place.

'Found it okay then,' Jack said from the open door as Stanley approached. He was wearing tracksuit trousers and a white polo T-shirt that clung to his bulky frame. His physical presence was imposing.

'Evidently, yes,' said Stanley.

Jack held open the door. Stanley entered into a hallway decorated in pale pink with a floral carpet. He noticed a display of dried flowers on a wooden stand. The place felt homely but dated. He definitely sensed a woman's touch.

They skirted awkwardly around one another as Jack closed the front door. Stanley wondered whether it was just he who sensed a shift in their dynamic. This domestic setting and Jack's casual clothing sat so at odds with what had come before. The contrast between this and the formality of Jack's suits and dogged procedure caught Stanley off guard.

Stanley fought the urge to ask questions. His head whirred privately with thoughts.

'I've pulled out the most relevant files for you,' said Jack. 'Got a lockable filing cabinet to keep everything secure. But I thought it'd be easier for us to look at them in the dining room.'

The dining room was snug, with heavy wooden furniture that felt too big for it. A table was accompanied by a glass-fronted cabinet filled with Royal Doulton figurines and decorated crockery. Neat lace curtains hung over the windows.

Jack had stacked various dog-eared folders on the table. Stanley noted that several had scribbled labels on them. Their appearance didn't suggest any great overview or sophistication.

Jack's eagerness to crack on with the task at hand was obvious. He heaved himself onto one of the chairs and indicated where Stanley was to sit opposite.

They both reached for reading glasses.

There was no wedding ring on Jack's finger. Stanley had never noticed before. It hadn't seemed important. He wasn't sure why his surroundings should bring it to the forefront of his mind. It was the bungalow not feeling like a family home. Nor that of a bachelor. Instead, it gave the impression of Jack being an intruder or imposter.

The lack of small talk or chit-chat suited Stanley just fine. Much safer to stick to the business at hand.

'I've been thinking about the crime scene,' he said. 'That's where I would prefer to start from.'

'Absolutely,' said Jack, rifling through the stack of folders. 'Here we are. This one should contain all the details.'

He began to thumb through a chaotic bundle of pages.

Should didn't sound too confident.

'Let's start with the post-mortem report,' Jack said. 'It outlines time of death between a window of time on that afternoon. Which fits in with Ashleigh having been at home with the Rainsfords before they went out that day, and when Jacinta found her later in the summerhouse. Cause of death is listed as fatal head injury caused by a single blunt force trauma.'

'So a single blow to the head.'

'Yes,' said Jack.

'With a weapon?'

'There wasn't one found at the scene, so it's recorded as an unidentified object.'

'It doesn't sound like there's much to go on.'

'Exactly. You can look at the forensics documents in your own time. Not that there's anything of use in there. The only thing they did was confirm that there'd been nobody in the vicinity who wasn't already known to Ashleigh. Nothing that couldn't be accounted for.'

Stanley scratched his chin. 'Nothing at the scene to suggest an altercation?'

'No.'

'Footprints?'

'There'd been a dry spell, so the ground was hard. Even the weather hadn't been helpful to us.'

So as far as Stanley could see, the perpetrator could have approached from either the house or the gate at the end of the garden. And the potential suspects all looked to be someone that Ashleigh had known. Of which one of whom had struck her forcefully on the head.

'Thoughts?' asked Jack.

Stanley wasn't sure. He was reluctant to commit to any initial speculations. 'What strikes me is how small Ashleigh's world seemed. She'd moved out of the family home where she'd lived with her stepfather after her mother died. Then her focus had been on looking after Sophie. Employed by Oliver and Jacinta.'

'I'm not sure that's unusual these days,' said Jack. 'She wasn't the only person to have a small circle around her.'

Stanley hadn't got a handle on Ashleigh as a person. At the moment, she was nothing more to him than an abstract idea. Not a *human* at all. He made a mental note to try and construct a better picture of her.

'Social media?' asked Stanley.

'All the usual accounts. But she wasn't a prolific user. You'll find her profile addresses in the paperwork. As far as I know, they're still active. Nobody requested their closure.'

Stanley would look in his own time.

From beyond the net curtains, a dustcart pulled into view. In its wake were two men in fluorescent orange workgear noisily pulling wheelie bins up to the rear of the vehicle. Their voices exchanged banter against the roar of the engine, but the words they spoke were lost in the noise. Stanley watched as the bins lifted on mechanical arms, their lids flapping as the contents emptied into the belly of the truck. He wondered at the disposal of everyday waste, the bi-product of unthinking consumerism.

His mind had drifted.

The fleeting burst of activity beyond the rose bushes rumbled slowly out of view, leaving behind a sense of stillness.

A collar dove coo-ed from a tree.

Jack was still talking as he rummaged through the files on the table. Stanley hoped he hadn't missed something important. He hadn't been listening at all. His mind had caught on what Jack had said in passing. About modern life creating small circles. And wondering whether that was true of the two of them sat at the table. He was in danger of veering completely off track.

A strange sensation crept upon him. It was a word, really. Not so much a feeling.

And the word was *vulnerable*.

*Classic Auto Repair*s was located on an industrial estate and housed in a metal unit with a retractable roller frontage. There was allocated parking at its front marked out by white lines.

Jack had, once again, insisted on driving them both.

From their stationary position, the whirr of electric tools drifted over the muffled thump of music.

'So this is where Lorenzo Conti works?' asked Stanley.

'Yes,' said Jack. 'He got an apprenticeship when he left school, and they employed him as mechanic when he was qualified. His family own a restaurant in town.'

'Italian?'

'Uh-huh.'

'You described his relationship with Ashleigh as on-off...'

'Yes, from all accounts their dating was a bit rocky. They both went to a local gym. But apart from that, I could never see what they had in common. He's got a bit of a track record. Not always been on the right side of the law.'

Stanley thought he detected an edge to Jack's voice. A tone that he wasn't familiar with. It sounded as if Lorenzo's card had been marked.

'Opposites attract,' said Stanley.

Jack grunted. His guard appeared to be going up, almost as if invisibly he was putting up a shield in preparation for meeting Lorenzo again.

'Was Ashleigh the same age as him?'

'He's four years older,' said Jack, again his voice suggesting disapproval.

They approached over the tarmac to be greeted by a stocky middle-aged mechanic in greasy overalls. He was wiping a spanner with a cloth.

'A split-screen VW camper,' said Stanley, looking up at the orange and white van raised above a pit.

Jack looked incredulously at him.

'An original,' said the ruddy-faced man. He stepped over to turn down the radio, before looking at Jack. 'Not here on new business?'

'No,' said Jack. 'This is Stanley Messina. He's reviewing the murder case of Ashleigh James.'

'I see.'

'We'd like to have a quick chat with Lorenzo. Is he here?'

'You've just missed him. He's out doing errands. Won't be back for some time...'

*

Lorenzo Conti crouched behind a desk in the office. He was lithe and agile from all the boxing at the gym. His instincts were sharp like a wild animal.

Through the internal window, he could see a conversation happening. It was the same copper as before. He'd seen him pull up outside. Been quick to tell his boss and make a quick exit.

His boss would understand. He was good like that.

Not like the police.

They never understood.

He looked at the arrogant detective who'd investigated Ashleigh's death. He made his skin crawl. Just remembering the patronising way in which he'd spoken to him. Talking down to him like a child.

He'd like to have a chance to go a few rounds with him in the ring. Be good to see if he thought himself better than him then.

The copper was leaving now.

He didn't recognise his sidekick. Something about him didn't look quite the same as the other one.

What did they want?

Couldn't they let him move on with his life?

Couldn't they just let Ashleigh rest in peace…

CHAPTER 6

Jacinta strolled attentively up the aisle, holding the bottle of champagne with a starched white napkin around its neck.

'Champagne, Sir? Champagne, Madam?'

It was the point in pre-flight procedures when things were busy. Her small team were ensuring that everything was prepared for the hours ahead. Industriously toiling behind the scenes.

The clientele at the front end of the plane expected luxury. They were paying a handsome premium for the service, to be waited on hand and foot in this cocoon. Their loyal business was vital to the ongoing survival of the airline.

She had got used to the commute from Clifton Sands to Gatwick airport, traipsing her small wheeled hand luggage behind her.

The plane still sat on the tarmac, but through the oval windows she could see that the vehicles used to transport suitcases and bags were pulling away. The hold was being secured.

This was one of her routes. A flight to New York.

The passage was one that attracted an array of customers. In addition to the regulars flying on business, there were often celebrities or minor royals. There were those too who had scraped together life savings for a once in a lifetime experience.

Jacinta treated them all equally. Showering them with a deference that such a price tag demanded.

The captain in his winged lapelled jacket and hat had acknowledged her cordially on his way to the flightdeck. She had worked hard to get to her position of responsibility.

Moving back towards the galley kitchen, she glanced back down the plane to economy class. The rows and rows of crammed seats were filling with an impatient queue of travellers, who would sit with their knees to their chests for the journey.

Her early flying years had seen her employed by a budget airline on which there'd been no business or first class. Not one to rest on her laurels, she'd progressed to another carrier who had the opportunity for her to progress.

It wasn't, she knew, a respected job in everyone's eyes. But it had never stopped filling her with excitement and a sense of fulfilment. In dressing in her pristine uniform, she liked to think that she was portraying a sense of glamour. However demanding her passengers might be, she wore a smile upon on her painted lips.

Now, of course, she didn't need to work at all. How many times had Oliver told her that? They didn't need her to earn money, he'd insisted.

She wasn't sure he ever completely understood. It wasn't just about the money. It was her identity.

'Don't you want to stay at home with Sophie?' he'd asked when their daughter had been a baby.

Looking back, she wondered why she hadn't asked him the same question.

Why couldn't she have it all? Why should she have to give up the profession she loved just because she'd had a child?

Jacinta had spent considerable time manifesting her present life. She thought back on the vision boards she'd built back then, festooned with images of the person she saw herself being. She'd pinned the board with affirmations. A wealthy husband. A stellar career. A beautiful child.

That board had long gone. To be replaced by the trappings of the things she'd desired.

She moved in higher circles these days. Still, however, she strove to be more than just an adjunct to her husband and his empire. Every dream comes with compromise. She'd grown to understand that.

The plane gave a little jolt. It was taxi-ing backwards.

Jacinta rallied her team to ensure that everything was in place for final checks before departure. She watched possessively as her colleagues efficiently and calmly ensured that seatbelts were fastened and that overhead lockers were secured firmly. She walked back and forth with reassuring nods and smiles.

They were soon pulling up to the side of the runway.

A gentle hush descended as the plane edged forward. Jacinta took her designated seat and clipped her seatbelt clasp together and tightened the belt. As the roar of the engines raised, her heartbeat raced. She had never tired of the thrill of take-off. She loved the drag upon her as they thundered down the tarmac, gathering pace.

The lights of the airport shot by the windows.

And then, the nose of the plane lifted. Gradually, and always miraculously, the weight of the plane rose above the ground in a thrilling incline. Into the sky and banking.

Jacinta laced her manicured hands together. The ultimate picture of composure. And smiled to herself.

Often, much like the crew behind the blinking spread of dials in the cockpit, Jacinta would switch into auto-pilot mode during a flight. The routines by which drinks and meals were served had become so ingrained, that frequently they required no thought at all. It hardly ever crossed her mind that they were hurtling through the sky at several thousand feet.

Today, however, she felt a strange sensation of tripping over her own self. The role she usually slipped into so easily seemed nothing more than a pretence.

She busied herself with tasks, hoping that her colleagues wouldn't notice anything different.

As she fussed with hot drinks at the galley kitchen, the chiffon scarf around her neck suddenly felt too tight. Her face became hot. Was she in danger of having a panic attack? The thought lurched her further towards losing control.

Breathe, she told herself. Just take a moment. And breathe.

The memories were flooding back. From behind that barrier that she shouldered shut so determinedly, they were seeping back in horrific clarity…

It was a summer's day. The sun sparkled in the sky. Waves lapped lazily onto the pebbled beach. Yes, she thought, they'd been the model family. Just for once. A shining moment of how others lived their lives. At least on the surface.

Jacinta tugged her scarf with a nail.

The glorious image in her mind's eye began to twist. There were voices now, crowding in insistently, giving their opinions. She could hear Sophie protesting. 'No daddy! No!' Her plump little fingers trying to pull her father back. But it wasn't a fair match. He was so much bigger and stronger. He was always going to win the struggle.

Sophie's sobs rang in her ears.

She'd looked to her mother for comfort and reassurance. But cut her down with calls for the young woman. 'Ashleigh,' she'd said. 'I want Ashleigh…'

The plane bumped. Not uncommon to encounter turbulence. It never usually fazed her. Although, right now her knees were in danger of buckling beneath her.

Her heart pounded in her chest.

She was walking up to the summerhouse now. Every time that moment returned to her, she saw it in slow motion. Her vision grew blurred at the edges, moving forward in tunnel vision. The sounds of the garden – birdsong, a passing jet – grew muffled and distant. Only the sound of air escaping her lungs.

As her hand encased the handle, she saw the crumpled shape through the glass within. At first, she'd mistaken her for being asleep. A thought quickly dismissed because of the way in which her hair splayed out across her vacant expression.

Jacinta had shaken her. Held her cold shoulders and shook her like a rag doll.

But her head lolled backwards.

She wouldn't be alone with her for long. Obviously, their

home – and life – was about to shatter. They would be the object of gossip and scrutiny.

That's when, she supposed, instinct kicked in. She steeled herself. Time was not on her side. Her eyes darted back to the house. There were decisions to be made. And quick…

'Jacinta?'

She blinked. Standing before her was one of her fellow flight attendants. He was one she liked. A gentle man who lived in Brighton with his husband.

'Are you okay?' he asked.

'I might have a migraine coming on,' she lied.

He fussed around her offering water and insisting she sat down, which she reluctantly obeyed. She would be fine. Just needed a moment. Absolutely nothing to worry about…

Having given herself a strong speaking to, Jacinta had rallied swiftly. Back on her feet, she was back at the helm, sensing relief from her team that her recovery had been quick. To manage everything with a pair of hands down was a challenge.

Jacinta received confirmation that they were in their final descent towards New York City, and the latter routines of the flight kicked in. A last opportunity for hospitality and possible duty-free sales before the final tidy up began.

An announcement over the tannoy from the flightdeck raised hopes that the captain would be directed over the city skyline. It was dark now, but the panorama would be illuminated by the constant blazing lights. An excited hum rippled through the passengers.

Jacinta was glad to be reaching their destination. There had been no unexpected issues, apart from her own minor wobble, to dwell on after landing.

She wondered what had triggered it. That horrible feeling of uncontrollable panic. It was probably a concern about losing control.

Ever since she'd heard again from DI Jack Sheppard, it had niggled her that things were slipping away from her. Just when her home and life seemed to be re-gaining some order. It would sound harsh, she knew, if she said that to anyone else. But it was the truth. What had happened to Ashleigh was a terrible thing, and yet somehow life had to go on.

Jack Sheppard's presence only drew them all back to that unsettling time. A reminder that the fabric of their existence might still be unravelled by the tugging of loose threads.

The team took their seats again as the plane descended towards the parallel lights of the runway. Whilst the others engaged in sociable small-talk, Jacinta sat quietly with her thoughts.

She removed a compact from her pocket and examined her face in its round mirror. Her eyes looked tired in its reflection.

It had only recently occurred to her what she found disconcerting about DI Sheppard. Yes, she'd always considered him abrupt and opinionated. He had always been rough around the edges. Only on being confronted by him again did it strike her how unreceptive he was to her charms. Men, in her opinion, were often easily won over. It wasn't the done thing to acknowledge, but looks had been important in climbing the ladder. Men liked to be flattered. To be shown attention.

No, she thought, Jack Sheppard hadn't shown a flicker of interest at all…

She squinted at the mirror. There were a couple of lines between her brows. The consequence of worrying and frowning. Fine lines too laced beneath her eyes. Thankfully, the cost of botox wasn't a concern. She must book an appointment at the clinic. Keeping oneself presentable was a necessity these days. No longer a choice.

She thought of Sophie's youth. She wondered what she was doing now. Was Bernadette getting her ready for bed? Telling her a story?

Funny how having a child made you more aware of age. That ever-creeping ascending number.

Jacinta reminded herself that she wanted it all. Why

shouldn't she? She'd worked hard for it. Only in down moments, like these few minutes, did she consider that she was missing out on Sophie growing up. That somebody else was delighting at her significant milestones. Another person building a bond with her.

She powdered her face, dabbing the sponge across her cheeks. Not too young to consider filler. Her lips too might benefit from being plumped she thought as she pouted.

Her face loomed large. She scrutinised it, trying to recognise the woman beneath the surface.

She had made her choices.

Simple as that.

Life is all about making decisions.

Choices and decisions.

And as the wheels made contact with the ground of another country, Jacinta snapped shut her compact.

CHAPTER 7

The unpredictability of British summer weather had, for once, fallen on the right side of clement.

Stanley seized the opportunity to stretch his legs, setting off through the streets on foot. Whilst his mind churned over the case at hand, he reminded himself to appreciate his surroundings. Most of the large houses had been converted into flats but many still retained impressive frontages. He noticed the details of bygone architecture. Important, he'd come to learn, to appreciate the small things.

He paused for a moment to marvel at the blooms of a hydrangea over a front garden wall. A honeysuckle scrambled up the building filling the air with a sweet scent.

Joy was to be found in simple pleasures. Things he'd once taken for granted. Until, of course, they'd been snatched away.

He moved on towards a pub located on one of the roads running parallel to the seafront. It was decorated with window boxes and hanging baskets of garish blooms. A smattering of customers sat at aluminium chairs and tables on the pavement, soaking up the afternoon sunshine.

Stanley's eyes adjusted as he stepped inside. The interior was welcoming. A light airiness made it feel unthreatening.

Jack stood already waiting with a half empty glass. Something about his posture suggested someone who was no stranger to propping up bars.

'Are you an ale or lager man?' he asked.

'Lager,' said Stanley. 'Although never on work hours.'

'So just a mineral water?'

'Thank you.'

'We're a bit early, I think,' said Jack. 'Gives us a chance to have a chat about how things are going.'

Stanley wondered how many of Jack's workdays had concluded in such places. Chewing over the details of whatever case he'd been working on at the time.

The thought made him shudder. What was it people said about somebody walking over their grave?

'Too on display if we sit outside,' said Jack. 'We'll be able to see if we sit near the window.'

They slid into seats that gave the vantage point they needed. The view was clear.

'Are you sure he'll be here?' asked Stanley.

'As sure as I can be,' said Jack. 'Either way, it gives us a chance to review your initial observations. Was it useful looking at the case files?'

'A bit overwhelming, to be honest. Going to take me some time to process months of information gathering.' He didn't want to say that the documentation had been raggedly put together. There'd been a scatter gun approach, to say the least. Quite easy to jump to a conclusion that logical leads might not have been pursued or overlooked entirely. 'What struck me from the paperwork was any sense of motive. That's what I've been mulling over.'

Jack sipped his beer. 'I'd like to hear your take on it. Be interesting to get your perspective without me clouding your judgement.'

'To begin with, I've been wondering whether anyone could have benefited from Ashleigh's death in anyway. Say, for example, was there some kind of material or purely financial gain that could be made by killing her. This looks unlikely based on the evidence in the files. As far as I could see she had no wealth. Her career as a nanny didn't pay much. I only wondered about her mother…'

'Yes?' said Jack.

'You said that she'd died from a long-term condition. But left nothing to her daughter when she died?'

'From memory, there was nothing to leave Ashleigh. I suppose the house was in joint names with Reece before her mother died. We have nothing to suggest that Ashleigh was aggrieved with her step-father in any way.'

'And yet, we know that she moved out of the family home to take up residence with the Rainsfords. Which raises the question as to what prompted this decision. Purely a chance to pursue her career? Or an opportunity to escape?'

'Escape? What from?'

'I don't know,' said Stanley. 'I'm just making suggestions.'

Jack looked into Stanley's eyes. How different from the times he'd eyeballed him in the past.

'Anything else?' Jack asked, hopefully.

'Well, either I'm looking at a material gain from the wrong perspective, or the motive is something else entirely. I don't know enough about her relationship with Lorenzo Conti to make a call on that one yet.' Hopefully he would soon have more information on that front.

Jack leapt quickly on this line of thinking. 'What sort of motive might he have had?'

A host of words jumped to the forefront of Stanley's mind. Betrayal? Jealousy? Revenge? They were all big words. Big words that currently had nothing to substantiate them. At the moment, they would simply be empty accusations.

'Relationships can be complicated,' said Stanley.

Jack grunted, clearly finding the response inadequate.

Stanley continued: 'Which leads to the nature of her relationship with her employers: Oliver and Jacinta. And again, I haven't got sufficient information to draw any conclusions. Not out of the realms of possibility that there might be frictions working and living under the same roof. Although, stretching that theory to the conclusion of murder would be pushing it a bit far.'

'Sounds like you're lining up the key players,' said Jack.

'Not sure I'd put it like that. But yes, in a way. I'm trying to build up a stronger picture. There's a balance, isn't there? Between speculating on possible motives and ensuring that all are treated innocently until proven guilty.'

Jack looked to be holding his tongue, indicating that he saw investigating in entirely the opposite direction. Stanley didn't need to be reminded of that.

'I haven't got a sense of who Ashleigh was as a person yet. Reading about her in the case files felt kind of…' he struggled to find the right word. 'Abstract?'

Jack nodded. 'Murder has a way of doing that.'

'It's as if she's got lost in it all. That in being labelled simply as *victim* she's been stripped of her emotions. What were her dreams? What made her tick?'

'I guess that our attention focused more on who the killer might be,' said Jack. 'And besides, Ashleigh's world looked to be very small.'

That didn't mean her dreams might not have been big, thought Stanley.

Jack cast his gaze out on to the street. It was difficult to keep his attention focused on one topic for too long, always jumping from one thing to another. Whether this was just his nature or a product of spinning too many plates at work, Stanley couldn't say. Only that this habit added to an increasing concern that might explain why the original inquiry had stalled.

Stanley attempted to pull the conversation back on track. Not to lose the thread:

'When you say small world… What do you mean by that?'

Jack dragged his eyes back to the table. There was a petulance about him that Stanley hadn't encountered before. An impatience to move on. 'Kids these days have their heads filled with possibilities. At school, they're told they can do anything if they work hard enough. Just so long as they get the grades. They watch online clips of influencers and believe they'll be the next to hit the big time. They expect all the doors to be opened to them. That somehow, they're entitled to it.'

What 'it' was, Stanley didn't know. Truth be told, he wasn't sure Jack was talking of Ashleigh at all. The bitter edge in his voice suggesting more of personal experience.

'Looks to me,' said Jack, 'that perhaps she had a bit of a reality check. Having left school, it looks as if she quickly lost touch with her circle of friends. Maybe the reality of living in a small town with few opportunities hit her? Not to mention what impact her mother's death had on her. By the time she was working for the Rainsfords, she looks to have become pretty isolated, wouldn't you say?'

Stanley nodded. He thought of the rambling house, and the little girl with her nanny. How often, he wondered, had the two of them been on their own? Only having one another for company.

Vulnerable.

It was that word again.

'It makes me wonder,' said Stanley, 'how she looked at the world. If her view of it might've been skewed by those around her.'

'Do you mean she might've been susceptible? To what?'

Stanley sensed they were going round in circles. Stuck in a loop of hypothetical questions.

'I just wondered who might have had her ear. Who she might have been influenced by.'

'I'm not sure how much we considered that. The picture pointed towards a girl who was headstrong and independent. The Rainsfords must've trusted her enough to leave their daughter in her care.' A crestfallen expression fell upon Jack's face, almost hound dog. 'It's what so frustrating about it all. To have such a small circle of possible suspects and not to be able to pin anything on one of them.'

Yet again, Stanley rankled at his turn of phrase. He considered challenging it, but decided against it. For now, he would firmly view Jack as a paying client. Quite frankly, he had bills to pay and couldn't afford to lose the work.

'I think I need to look more closely at the files to read up on what follow-up was carried out on confirming the alibis,' said Stanley.

'You're welcome to do that. Not sure what good it will do you though. Everything seemed to be pretty watertight.'

'Seemed' offered a tiniest glimmer of possibility.

Stanley thought of the stack of paperwork. It was hard to know where to begin. The cliché of a needle in a haystack sprang to mind.

With this at the forefront of his brain, he asked: 'Is there anything in particular that I ought to know about the evidence? Anything in all that documentation that might be important or significant?'

'There's one thing,' said Jack.

'Yes?'

'There's the issue of her locket. Ashleigh's, I mean.'

'A locket?'

Just then, Jack's phone began to vibrate and flash on the table. He snatched it up and looked at the caller ID. 'Sorry, I've got to take this...'

As he slid away from the table, clasping the phone to his ear, Stanley felt intrusive as he heard snatches of a one-sided conversation. There was an unfamiliarity to the tone of his voice. Something softer about it. Soon, Jack was too distant to overhear, his voice lost in the surrounding chatter of the pub.

Stanley busied himself with a ratty coaster, trying not to look at Jack's harried posture. He was frowning. He paced back and forth as he spoke to the person at the other end of the line, until eventually the call ended and he returned to the dregs in his pint glass at which he looked sadly. Another one, clearly, was being considered.

No explanation or apology for the interruption was offered. He looked to be caught up in his own head.

'Where were we?' he said, physically shaking his attention back into his body. It was the scatter gun again.

'You were saying about a locket? That belonged to Ashleigh?'

Stanley's hope of steering things back on track quickly

evaporated as once again Jack's focus moved to something that had caught his eye outside.

'Bingo!' he said, his spirits suddenly appearing to lift.

Stanley looked. Along the opposite pavement, a dark-haired young man in black trousers and a white shirt was hurrying in a half-jog. He was recognisable from photos in the case files. Jack had been right. His information had proved correct. Last time, it was clear that the man had given them the slip.

Today, however, Lorenzo Conti would not escape them.

CHAPTER 8

Lorenzo sweated in the late afternoon heat. He could already hear his father's voice ringing in his head, complaining at his tardiness. He wiped the perspiration from his forehead. It was a well-worn routine he'd followed for years. Nothing that required any particular attention. He certainly wasn't aware of the streetscape around him, not giving the pub across the road a thought.

Having finished his day at the garage, he'd crammed in an express session at the boxing gym, going hard at the punchbag as his mind fought trawling through everything again. He'd gone at it like a wild animal, losing track of time as he frequently did.

It was how he'd learnt to cope with things. To try and ensure that every minute of every day was busy. Keeping himself away from those who would drag him into trouble. His mother always said that he was easily led.

Always better, he found, to be running slightly late for everything. No opportunity then for the devil to make work for idle hands.

Amici Italiani was a small restaurant tucked back from the promenade. Its name was painted proudly on its front window beneath a red sun canopy which was bookended by two Italian flags.

Lorenzo was the second generation of an immigrant family. His grandparents had moved to the UK from Sicily in search of a better life.

He bounded in through the entrance. The lights were never

turned on until the sign on the door was flipped to 'open', giving the tables with their gingham tablecloths a deserted look. Candles from the previous night had burned down into waxy blobs, all waiting to be replaced before the next sitting.

The restaurant didn't have a large number of covers. It had, however, become something of a local institution, popular with both the residents of Clifton Sands and many a returning visitor to the town. The brick arches within and the traditional art and photos on the wall were authentic. Not at all the pastiches of the cookie-cutter giants who threatened to steal business away.

A glow came from the circular window in the door to the kitchen. Lorenzo nudged it open and smelt the fragrant sauces bubbling already on the hobs.

'I'm here, Papa,' he said.

'You're late!' came the regular reply.

Lorenzo knew it was best to leave his father to his culinary preparations. His mother frequently bemoaned their similar headstrong personalities. She chastised them for clashing. Yet always sought to have them fight for her undivided attention.

She wouldn't arrive until later, to take her place behind the miniature counter, perching on a stool to oversee the proceedings.

As a boy, Lorenzo had proudly learnt the ropes. Being an only child, he'd felt the overwhelming affection from his extended family. There had always been whispers that his parents had wanted more children, but it hadn't happened. The consequence of complications during his birth, apparently. This had only amplified his sense of being special. The apple of his mother's eye.

He kicked into autopilot, setting about polishing the cutlery and glasses before laying the tables. It was something he'd done since a young boy. Back then, of course, they'd dressed him in a little waiter's outfit. Much to the delight of many a regular customer. He'd always delighted in the theatre of it all. The buzz of a busy service.

It was the same excitement he discovered later in cars, the roar of an engine. Much, of course, to the disapproval of his father, who had naturally seen his son as an heir and successor to *Amici Italiani*. To follow the path laid down by his grandfather. To continue the tradition.

Sometimes, Lorenzo found himself frowning at the prints that hung on the walls. The scenes of olive groves and remote villages jarred against the traditional seaside town he'd always known as home. That heritage and treasured sense of homeland which seemed to flow so easily in the blood of his family, didn't resonate as strongly with him. It was as if he was caught somewhere in the middle of the two. A no-man's land in which he was neither one thing nor another. On days like today, the sun transformed his skin into a dark hone. He remembered how Ashleigh, who's complexion was so pale, had marvelled at the comparison between them.

'You're so lucky to have a family,' she'd said. It was something she'd said a lot, as if to constantly remind him or convince him.

He had felt lucky. And yet also silently constrained. Both a blessing and a curse.

It was when he thought of Ashleigh, that he remembered that she'd brought out the best and the worst in him. He'd never really believed in love at first sight. Not until he'd met her. At which, the spark was so strong he felt it as a physical ache in his chest. A spark which as time progressed, frequently flared up into an inferno of emotions. The passionate latin blood, a flowing link to his ancestors.

Having prepared the restaurant, he popped his head into the kitchen and acknowledged his father before returning to front of house and turning on the lights. He put on the traditional music. And suddenly, a tucked away corner of Clifton Sands became a little part of the Mediterranean.

Lorenzo flipped the sign to 'open' before turning his attention to the reservations book. Only a couple of tables to pop reserved signs on.

He heard the door open but didn't turn immediately.

'Will be right with you,' he called.

There was nothing about the lack of response that raised any concern with him. Even when he turned, his eyes took some time to register who had entered.

He froze.

It was the copper. And a man with him. Another policeman?

'Table for two, please.'

Lorenzo felt the fire ignite in his bones. No reason to turn away custom but having narrowly avoided an anticipated interrogation at the garage, it was unlikely that they were here simply for the pasta. To encroach upon his family territory made him uncomfortable. It had taken months of repair work to convince them that he hadn't permanently gone off the rails. He didn't need anything that would give them reason to doubt him again.

He tried to avoid eye contact as he approached them. 'You're here to eat?'

'Yes,' said the man he was familiar with. He'd forgotten how tall and broad he was. A quick glance reminded him of his rugged face. Why did all policemen have a similar look to them?

Lorenzo held out his arm to a table in the corner. As the pair moved towards it, he looked at the copper's companion. His skin looked similar to his own.

'You remember me, Lorenzo?' said the policeman. 'Jack Sheppard.'

Lorenzo stiffened his spine. He thought again of wanting to fight this man in the ring. 'I do. You thought I had something to do with Ashleigh's murder.'

Jack Sheppard shook his head. 'Now, that's not how it was.' His gruff voice managed to sound patronising. That's how he'd always spoken to him. Looking down his nose from his high horse. 'We tried to catch up with you at *Classic Autos*…'

Lorenzo didn't reply.

Jack continued: 'This is Stanley Messina. He's a private

investigator. I've asked him to review the investigation into the case.'

The fire in his blood began to rise. He could feel his face growing red. How dare they come into his workplace and family life. What right did they have to drag him back into it all?

The other man – this Stanley Messina – interjected gently. 'I want to do the right thing by Ashleigh. Until the person who killed her is convicted, there'll be no justice for her.'

'That's all any of us want,' said Lorenzo.

'Doesn't look good on you if you carry on running away and hiding from us,' said Jack.

Lorenzo noticed a flash of irritation on Stanley's face. Had there just been a kick of shins under the table?

'I can't guarantee that a review will reach an outcome,' said Stanley, 'but there'll be a better chance if you can work with us. That's what we want, isn't it?' He looked to Jack's rugged face across the table, who nodded.

It would take more than a few soft words to change his opinion.

'Drinks?' he asked.

'Just water for the table, please,' said Stanley, quickly. Prompting a sulky expression on Jack's face. Not happy with being spoken for? Or hoping for something stronger than water?

When he returned with a water jug, the two men were studying their menus. Surely this method of investigation was unconventional.

He was torn. No way did he want to spend any time with the detective, facing his assumptions and judgements. But, on the other hand, if there was any chance that it might move things on, he had to consider it. He couldn't deny that he was curious. What had prompted this revival into the case? Had any new information come to light?

'They treated her very badly,' he found himself saying. 'They wouldn't let me see her. Keeping her behind the walls of that big house of theirs…'

'The Rainsfords?' asked Stanley. 'Is that who you mean?'

The fire was simmering again. It always burnt when he thought of that family. 'Oliver Rainsford is a nasty piece of work. He's slimy.'

'Your insight could make all the difference,' said Stanley.

'But will you listen this time?'

He sensed Jack Sheppard bristle.

'Yes,' said Stanley. 'You have my word.'

Later that evening, Stanley walked alone along the seafront promenade, hoping that he would be able to keep his promise to Lorenzo Conti.

A high pressure system had settled over the south coast. The English Channel was smooth. In the distance a container ship slid along the horizon, whereas in the foreground a group of paddleboarders propelled themselves energetically to nowhere in particular.

This time of year, the daylight lingered. Only those out late, or those with sea view hotel rooms, got to see the pretty arcs of lights twinkling between the Victorian lampposts or the illuminated ferris wheel.

Stanley thought of the fractured snippets they'd garnered from Lorenzo during the meal as he returned to their table. He hadn't wanted to speak much. Didn't feel comfortable with family close around. That seemed fair enough. Maybe he was a man of few words anyway.

That Ashleigh had been his girlfriend was not new information. He was, he'd said, still in contact with her best friend, Bernadette. But his obvious dislike of the Rainsfords hadn't made this easy. Not with Bernadette now under their roof. He worried for her. Just as Reece had expressed a similar concern.

'He's got convictions,' Jack had told Stanley again, out of Lorenzo's earshot. 'Has a reputation for getting into fights.'

Stanley would draw his own conclusions.

That's why he'd insisted on walking on his own, turning down Jack's offer of joining him.

The ferris wheel began to turn.

Stanley thought of Ashleigh and those around her. Things happen to other people in life. Unexpected things. Terrible things. Shocking things. Sad things. And yet, Stanley thought, you don't believe that they will happen to you. Until they do.

He wished his thoughts could be contained to the question of who had killed Ashleigh. He should be focused on trying to make some sense of it all. Not letting his mind drift to the man who'd sat devouring a pizza in front of him. Wondering what his story really was. Thinking of ideas that he'd like to share with him.

Trying to fathom how Jack Sheppard could be the same demon he'd harboured in his head for so long. The shadow that had triggered all the things that one never imagines could ever happen…

CHAPTER 9

Oliver Rainsford's inbox was full of unread emails. He liked to begin his day by rattling off as many responses as he could before his schedule really kicked in. He sipped his coffee and frowned. There was a lot of junk. Other companies trying to sell products and services.

He was always the first to arrive, believing that it was true about the early bird catching the worm. Over the years, he'd done his best to try and move with the times. Evolving, he knew, was the only way to survive.

It was why they'd moved to a larger space. A main open-plan office where the team could hot desk and collaborate, with a smaller meeting room and his own individual glass walled office. Of which, the glass came with benefits and downsides. Whilst allowing him to feel connected with his staff and keeping an eye on proceedings, it also made his own interactions entirely visible. Sometimes he felt like a goldfish in a bowl.

Oliver looked at the clock.

He was beginning to regret his choice of new personal assistant. She hadn't proved to be the best at timekeeping. Neither had her work ethic been strong.

He'd begun to wish he'd chosen the other candidate. A woman with a grey bob and flat shoes. But instead, he'd been blinded by a short skirt and attractive smile.

Perhaps he would have to have a quiet word with her in private. Just to make sure she understood what was expected of her…

*

'There are lots of cliches regarding education these days.'

'Such as?' asked Oliver.

The woman opposite him consulted her notepad. 'Knowledge is the new economy. Teaching is big business.'

'We've been around longer than those shallow soundbites,' said Oliver.

She blinked at him through thick lenses. He'd been repeatedly reassured that she was to be trusted as a feature writer. Her background wasn't in cut and thrust journalism. His team had vetted her and courted her aggressively.

'*Progressive Pathways* has been trading for over a decade,' she stated.

'Correct.'

Oliver realised that he'd forgotten her name. He hoped that he wouldn't need to say it.

'Was there a philosophy when you started the business?'

She was staying on message. Her list of potential topics for questions had been submitted prior to her visit.

'I wanted lifelong learning to be accessible to anyone at any age. I believed there was space for a 'one-stop shop' for combining careers guidance with necessary skills.' He said it as clearly as he could, hoping that his words had been picked up on the mobile phone on which she was recording the interview.

'You've been known to describe *Progressive Pathways* as like a department store for career development.'

'That's right. We offer online tools to help identify possible career interests. Some of these are general, others are psychometric and much more detailed. Then we have career interviews, bespoke CV writing services, work experience opportunities.'

'And specific training?'

'Yes. Both academic and vocational.'

'So you've monetised learning?'

She wasn't sticking entirely to the script.

'We provide a service,' said Oliver. 'The qualifications our clients achieve enable them to open doors that might never have been available to them. Arguably, the personal and financial longer-term benefits to them far outweigh the cost of purchasing our services.'

She was scribbling some notes to herself. Oliver tried to see what she'd written, but her handwriting was an indecipherable scrawl. Not to worry. They'd been promised final approval on the copy.

'It's a crowded market,' she said, sagely. 'Are you worried about competition?'

'We're the most 'joined-up' and user-friendly portal available. We pride ourselves on the quality of what we offer. The reviews and ratings online back this up. In many instances, we have lots of clients engage repeatedly with us.'

'So reputation is important.'

Oliver didn't like where the conversation was going. They'd done their best to keep the scandal at a distance. A murder could never be good for business.

He ran a finger under his collar which had suddenly started to feel tight.

'We operate under a strong set of principles and ethics,' said Oliver. 'Everything we do aims to put the client at the centre of our focus. We want them to trust us. To build a relationship with us. We want to see them fulfil their ambitions and dreams.'

'The business of success,' she said.

'A working title, perhaps?'

She looked to be considering it. But she didn't write it down. He would just have to wait and see.

Marcus Briggs, accountant to *Progressive Pathways*, wore a cheap crumpled white shirt and tatty looking grey and blue striped tie. Oliver didn't like the way he dressed. He never looked presentable. Surely, Oliver thought, he could afford clothes that looked more professional. But despite his sartorial misgivings, Oliver couldn't fault Marcus on his financial acumen. There wasn't a trick in the book he didn't know.

'How are things looking?' asked Oliver, conscious again of being in the goldfish bowl.

'On paper, the year-end accounts look above board and respectable.'

'But let's speak plainly. What about the reality?'

Oliver had grown to trust Marcus over the years. No private conversation held between them had ever come back to Oliver via other routes. His appearance suggested a man who watched the pennies. That's what you wanted in an accountant. Not somebody flash.

He'd go as far as saying that Marcus had become a trusted confidante.

'The latest audit was as clean as a whistle,' said Marcus. 'You're running a tight ship.'

'I sense a *but*?'

'It's the future projections that I'm concerned about.' He handed over a sheet of paper. It showed a five-year graph with increasing red ink as the time progressed.

'Have I seen this already?' asked Oliver. So much of what came through to him was only quickly glanced at. He thought again of the unopened emails stacking up. Too easy to overlook something important.

'I emailed you a copy.'

'Perhaps I just thought it was a paper exercise.'

'In theory, it is. The figures are purely speculative. You'll see I've factored in different scenarios.'

Oliver squinted at the information. 'They all look pretty bleak.'

'It's not your revenue, per se, that's the potential issue. If you keep attracting the same number of clients your income streams look solid.'

'Then why the difference?'

'It's your overheads. That's the problem. The cost of

everything has increased and continues to do so. In some respects, your delivery model is beginning to look old fashioned and outdated.'

Oliver respected the honesty despite it stinging. 'Outdated? In what ways?'

'Take advertising, for example. Your current methods of selling are heavily based in print media and radio. You haven't made the shift to targeted online advertising. Your social media presence is practically non-existent.'

'Isn't that just slinging mud against a wall?'

'You're showing your age,' said Marcus. 'It's the most effective and possibly cost-effective method of attracting new clients.'

'What else?'

'Your staffing model doesn't look productive. There's crossover between roles and multiple cases of where things could be automated. Which leads on to the question of office space.'

'You think we're paying too much for it?'

Marcus shrugged. 'I suppose it comes down to whether you need it at all. Remote working has become more acceptable now.'

'But what would we *be* without a physical space to define us? How would I know what everyone was *doing*?' The thought made him shiver.

Hadn't it not been so long ago that he'd felt at the forefront of it all? He'd been the young greyhound bounding ahead of the pack. It had felt as if there'd been everything to play for. The business had felt agile. Nothing at all like this marauding beast he was now tied to.

'What if we just stay with the status quo?' he asked.

Marcus looked at the sheet of paper clutched between Oliver's fingers. 'I don't think that's an option. Do you?'

Later that evening, Oliver looked at the London skyline from the balcony of their apartment on the river Thames. The property was one of the many things that the successful business had provided. It had served him well as a base during weekdays when the capital had been a natural nucleus for the quickly expanding company, growing fast beyond its initial fledgling status.

He looked at the planes with their landing gear down as they made their final approach into Heathrow. The sight of them always made him think of Jacinta. He admired her for following her passion to fly. She'd stood her ground on every occasion he'd suggested giving it up.

Some marriages, he knew, only worked because two people could never bear being apart. Doing everything together.

Theirs, however, thrived on being the opposite. It was strong because they appreciated one another's independence. Neither one was confined or constrained by the other. Not meaning that the bond between them wasn't powerful. It just wasn't tied so tightly that they couldn't pursue their individual ambitions.

Oliver stepped back into the sparse luxury of the apartment and poured himself a brandy. His mind was still mulling over his conversation with Marcus regarding the company accounts. How would he be able to justify his London life if there was no physical office to be seen at?

A photo of the three of them – husband, wife and child – stood proudly in a gilt frame on the expensive sideboard. The professional photographer had captured their perfect smiles. Sophie was clinging on to his hand, looking up at him adoringly. It made him think of that day on the beach. He'd insisted that she stay with her mother, but she'd tried to clamber over the pebbles to follow him. 'Go back,' he'd told her firmly. 'Go back…'

The year had taken its toll. Especially between him and Jacinta. He couldn't recall the last time they'd been physically close. Events had formed an icy barrier between them. They'd slipped into an unspoken agreement not to mention Ashleigh's name to one another. As if, perhaps, this avoidance might make things disappear. And yet, Oliver couldn't be sure that it hadn't only made things worse. Tip-toeing around a concealed landmine.

Had things felt so complicated in the past? He didn't think so.

Somehow, age was creeping up on him. No longer was he free of responsibilities. Funny, in a strange way, that his desire to escape the conformity of being a wage slave had resulted in more chains than he could ever have foreseen.

How much was he worth?

He didn't know. Somewhere along the way, he'd crossed a line over which he'd become a sum of fluctuating assets. The pursuit of freedom looked now to have become a battle to manage and protect what he'd accrued. To ensure that their lifestyle could be maintained.

Oliver looked at his phone. He wanted to re-read the messages from Jacinta. She said they'd been visited by the police. The same man who'd led the investigation into Ashleigh's murder. He didn't like the idea that things were being re-examined.

Perhaps, he thought, they would just keep on digging.

He could only hope that the truth was buried deep enough.

Jacinta put her key in the lock. The return flight to Gatwick had landed just before six pm.

The house was quiet. Bernadette would've read Sophie her bedtime story and tucked her in. However tempting it was to pop her head into her daughter's room, she knew that there was a chance of waking her.

The detective's reappearance in their lives had rattled her. She'd become complacent.

She wondered whether Oliver had too?

She had good mind to go and look in his study. To see whether any of the things she'd seen before still remained. Could she trust that he'd destroyed them?

But first, she would look to make sure that what she'd kept

was exactly where she'd hidden it. For that was her security. Her guarantee that she wouldn't fall the way others had in the past.

CHAPTER 10

Jack parked his car, as he'd done on countless occasions before, in the corner of the visitors parking area. The space was covered with dappled shade from overhanging branches. He liked the way the soft light flickered here. It was soothing. Sometimes he wound down the window and just listened to the birds calling to one another.

He was procrastinating, of course. Putting off the inevitable.

It had become almost a ritual. Taking a considered moment to galvanize himself.

He closed his eyes and put his head back against the seat rest. His mind drifted. His thoughts turned to how the re-investigation was going.

Stanley had shown himself to be pragmatic and level-headed. The manner in which he'd approached things so far had impressed him. For someone with no formal investigative training, he'd shown a natural ability for asking the most pertinent questions. It made Jack wonder whether he'd have been wary of him had he been a colleague. He didn't like to admit it, but he might've been jealous of Stanley's open mind and his easy way of speaking to people.

The force required a tougher edge than that.

Had Jack's time in it hardened him? Would he have grown as jaded if he'd followed another path?

The mottled sunlight was warm on his face. Shadows danced on his closed eyelids.

He wondered how Stanley was getting on looking through the evidence. He half hoped that his phone would ping with a message with an update or, better still, an invitation to join him in the process.

Jack opened his eyes and squinted. Now that Stanley was familiar with the case as a whole, the next steps would be to examine where things might have gone wrong in the investigation. That's what made Jack feel defensive. It reminded him of difficult conversations with the powers that be, justifying the methods he'd used, having to explain. The spotlight would again turn upon him.

Stanley – of all people – had more reason than anyone to be critical.

It was the reason for asking in him the first place, he supposed. That, and hoping to find some kind of forgiveness or redemption.

Procrastinating. Yes, most definitely procrastinating.

Jack forced himself to get out of the car.

The building had once been a formidable private residence. Since having being sold and converted into its current guise, several ugly additions had sprouted from its original grandeur. The sound of an extractor fan was accompanied by what seemed to be a constant whiff of vegetables being boiled.

Granted, *Cedar Woods* had little of the modern sheen that many of the others in Clifton Sands displayed. Jack had seen them all and collected each of their glossy brochures. And yet, there was something about this place. Something more homely. More human.

It was what she'd have chosen herself had she been able.

Through the porch, Jack entered the hallway where he signed in and pinned a visitors badge to his shirt. He was a familiar face to the staff. There were some residents, he knew, who were hardly visited at all. His heart sank at the sight of them alone. It only made him more determined to come here as regularly as possible.

There was a lift, but Jack always used the creaking stairs. The route was a well-trodden one. He could've done it with his eyes closed.

Making his way along the woodchip papered corridors, he

told himself once again that he'd done the right thing. It was fairer on her. To have carers on hand around the clock. A level of commitment that would've been impossible to manage alone.

However much he wrestled with it, Jack ultimately knew that she wouldn't have asked it of him.

The door was ajar.

He pushed it open gently, wondering at this point what he might find today.

She was slouched in a wingback chair looking tinier than he'd ever seen her before as if she was in danger of shrinking away to nothing at all. Her white-haired head had flopped onto her chest which heaved slowly in and out.

He was pleased that she was dressed neatly and her clothes were clean. It was obvious that her hair had been brushed.

His primary fear had always been that she might be neglected. But those concerns were unfounded at *Cedar Woods*.

He crouched down and wrapped his massive fingers softly on her fragile bony hand.

She opened her eyes blearily and tried to lift her head.

'Afternoon, Mum,' he said.

Her facial expression remained blank. These days, she showed nothing of what was going on inside. If, indeed, anything was going on at all. She showed no joy. Nor unhappiness. Just a façade like a mannequin.

She looked at him as he launched into his well-worn patter. He spoke of the weather. Both how it was and what the forecast looked like. He gave his observations on the neighbours. What he was planning to have for supper.

He tended to avoid the topic of politics, as much for his own sake as for hers. It frequently got his blood pressure up.

She didn't speak. Just moved her lips in a way that looked as if she was chewing on the words she might once had said.

Most days, she would stare emptily at him as he spoke until again she rested her head back down and closed her eyes. Then they would sit in companionable silence, with Jack hoping that she knew she wasn't alone.

In those quiet extended moments, Jack sat and contemplated in a way that his working life had never enabled him to.

He was relieved that she hadn't witnessed the failure of his final case. She'd always been so proud of his career. Although, it had crossed his mind, that this might have been down to his lack of family. She'd never said it, but he knew that she would've loved to have been a grandmother.

There were things he wondered whether he should've told her. One thing in particular. For his sake or hers he wasn't sure.

Too late now.

He looked at the golden cross on a chain that hung around her neck. He hoped that gave her peace.

At mid-afternoon, Stanley strode through the open gates to the parched grounds of the park. It was one of a number of entrance points around the perimeter and the closest, he'd been told, to his rendezvous spot.

Recreation grounds had always appealed to him. He appreciated the foresight of their designers in predicting how trees and shrubs would develop to fill the space over time. Here, the thick trunks and spreading canopies of the trees showed some considerable history. The paths zig zagged from formal gardens with exotic foliage to a neat bowling green, tennis courts and a hut serving as a café which looked to be a more modern addition.

The raucous shrieks of children playing indicated which direction he should head. As he drew closer, he saw an array of brightly coloured climbing apparatus and swings swarming with thrill-seeking little figures. The air buzzed with their frenetic energy.

She sat outside the wire fence that enclosed the play area. He recognised her petite frame despite her face being masked by a white cap and oversized sunglasses.

'I did wonder whether I might hear from you,' said Stanley, taking a seat beside her on the bench.

'Did you?' asked Bernadette.

'I wasn't sure if you'd been able to talk freely when we met before. And I thought you seemed a little anxious.'

From the mass of children, a frantic waving hand on a whirling contraption identified Sophie's presence. Bernadette mirrored the wave in reassurance.

'I can't be sure she won't tell them I've seen you,' she said. 'But if she does, I can spin them a story. Whose to say I didn't bump into you by chance? Or perhaps I met a friend who just happened to look like you. No laws against that. And besides, children are often mistaken by what they see, aren't they?'

Stanley saw that she'd already given it some thought since she'd messaged him. Too difficult to actually call him, he guessed. Never being sure what might be overheard within the walls of that house.

'You and Sophie have become close.'

'She's known me for a long time now. I'd often play with her when I caught up with Ashleigh. It's the main reason they asked me to take on the role after Ashleigh's death.'

'Jacinta and Oliver?'

'Yes. They thought it would be good to have someone she already knew.'

'Were you working as a nanny already elsewhere?' Stanley asked.

'No. I was employed at a nursery. It's attached to one of the private schools. It was where Ashleigh and I had undertaken our childcare placement. We worked together until Ashleigh got her job as Sophie's nanny.'

Stanley probed a little deeper. 'How did you feel about Ashleigh taking the job?'

'Nervous.'

'Nervous? For Ashleigh?'

'No,' said Bernadette. 'For me. I know it sounds selfish, but we'd always been at each other's side. People joked that we were joined at the hip. Almost as if we were one person.'

'And you told Ashleigh this?'

'We told each other everything. She said that I was being silly. It wasn't as if she was moving to the other side of the world and that we would see each other all the time.'

'And did you?'

She hesitated a fraction before replying, 'Yes.' Her voice suggesting more to it.

'Yes?'

'We *did* still see each other. It's just, that things weren't quite the same. Quite quickly, Ashleigh found life hard going. The money had won her over initially, but they'd never had a nanny before. It was as if they didn't know where the boundaries lay. There was always some kind of friction or drama going on between them.'

Stanley wasn't entirely surprised at this description. A brief trawl of the internet had returned many examples of forums in which nannies had discussed this very issue. A blurriness in regards to the lines of responsibility. Some had gone as far as describing themselves as slaves.

'So you saw a change in her?'

'All she wanted to do was talk about it. Asking me what I thought she should do. You'll be thinking that's what friends are for. Am I right?'

'I'm not here to judge,' said Stanley.

'I didn't really know how to handle it. I had run out of advice to give her. It was like we were going round in circles. I feel so bad now that I didn't do more to help. It had just become so draining. I feel guilty. It was the final straw, really. I just reacted.'

Stanley wasn't following. Her thoughts and words had leapt around.

'Sorry,' he said. 'I'm not sure I understand. To clarify, did you react to something in particular?'

He looked at her face. All he could see was the blur of children playing in the black reflection of her glasses.

'I don't know whether I should've told the police. I was scared. Being questioned terrified me. They were all so intimidating. And I'd promised Ashleigh…'

'Promised her what?'

'That I would keep it a secret.'

Stanley waited to see if she would divulge the information.

Eventually, she continued: 'Ashleigh told me that her period was late.'

'So she thought she might be pregnant?'

Bernadette nodded. 'She asked me, if she was, should she keep the baby or not? And I didn't know what to do. I was out of my depth. I told her that I missed our old friendship. Which she didn't like. Something snapped in that moment. It caught me off-guard. I was entirely side swiped. I'd been blindsided.'

'This was shortly before her death?'

'Literally the week before.'

'And Lorenzo would've been the father?' Stanley asked.

'I assumed so,' she said. 'Although, looking back, I never actually asked.'

Stanley wondered what new complexion this information put upon the information he'd been analysing in the case files. Were there aspects that he should look at again? How might things look different?

The young girl in pigtails was standing now, clutching the wire fence. She had tired of the equipment. Perhaps she was thirsty or wanted something to eat?

'I'll have to go,' said Bernadette.

'You've told me everything?' asked Stanley. 'There's nothing else?'

'Nothing else.' She got to her feet. 'Except…'

'Yes?'

'I want you to promise me that I'm safe in that house. Now that you're raking over things again. I'm not in any danger? Can you promise me that?'

Stanley, not being a person to make promises he couldn't keep, assured her that she could contact him at any time. Yet, with her eyes hidden behind her mirrored lenses, he couldn't say whether this made her feel any better or not.

CHAPTER 11

'Why the hell didn't she tell us this at the time?' Jack asked as he reverse parked. Finding a space in the centre of Clifton Sands was always difficult, especially during the summer season.

'She said that she'd felt intimidated by you,' said Stanley.

Jack huffed. 'Didn't she think that if Ashleigh *was* pregnant, that might be important?'

Stanley noted how neatly Jack had sidestepped the question of his perceived intimidating manner. Probably best not to poke the bear further.

'She said that she'd promised not to tell anyone. It was a secret between them. They'd been friends for a long time. They must've been a loyal to one another.'

The handbrake was applied fiercely.

'Besides,' Stanley added, 'wouldn't the post-mortem have revealed if she was pregnant?'

'Not necessarily. It would've been very early. Who knows, perhaps they weren't looking for it. They had no reason to. And these processes aren't always as thorough as they should be.'

Stanley had no experience in such things. Although, he knew from firsthand experience that formal procedures weren't always reliable. 'It's the fact that Ashleigh *thought* she might be pregnant, and that she was worried about it, that raises questions.'

'Wouldn't blame her for doubting whether Lorenzo Conti would make a great father. Having a baby with him would've tied him to her forever.'

'That's just one possibility.'

'What are you thinking?' Jack asked.

'Perhaps she was thinking about her career. How would she have managed to be a nanny if she had a baby of her own? Where would that have left her?'

'I can see your point. I don't think she could've relied on Lorenzo to support her. And would she have wanted to move back to living with Reece?'

'There's another obvious possibility, of course,' said Stanley. 'Just suppose that the baby wasn't Lorenzo's. Where would that leave us?'

Jack scratched his chin. 'It would definitely present some new motives. It might be worth thinking about. I guess it could change our opinion of Ashleigh. If she concealed this, what else might she have been hiding?'

Stanley didn't want to chase down things that couldn't be proved. Far too easy to blunder off down blind alleys. For now, he would keep an open mind.

They set off on foot to a humming area of town known for an array of thriving independent shops. Located a stone's throw from Clifton Sands train station, the streets had a quirky bohemian character about them. In addition to the smattering of charity shops, there were second-hand bookshops, a butcher, cafes, hairdressers and novelty stores. The scent of oriental food drifted from a Thai restaurant.

Stanley felt that Jack wasn't at ease. He could see his eyes devouring the streetscape. It was as if he was looking for trouble. He was noting every street drinker, every youth in a hoody, every suspicious looking interaction. Surprising, Stanley thought, how when one started to look, trouble could be seen everywhere.

'How's it going with the case files?' asked Jack.

'I'm trying to get them into some kind of order,' said Stanley, bravely.

'I see.'

'Fair to say that there are some lines of inquiry that weren't followed as thoroughly as they could've been.'

'You're expecting me to protest, aren't you?'

Stanley felt he had the upper hand. And he liked it. 'You're paying me to re-examine the case. Not to pass judgement on you.'

'Agreed. So which aspects of inquiry were lacking?'

'There are shortcomings, I think, in confirming the whereabouts and movements of suspects on the day of Ashleigh's murder. The cross-checking of verbal accounts doesn't look to have been very thorough. Also, the case files don't show much evidence of any exploration into the back stories of those involved. It makes me wonder whether there could be anything in their histories to link them in ways that haven't been considered.'

'*Back stories*,' Jack muttered under his breath. 'What is this? An Agatha Christie novel?'

Reece placed the needle on the revolving vinyl. A satisfying crackle came from the wall-mounted speakers, a moment of white noise above the street soundscape before the beat and bassline kicked in.

The shop was poky. Every available inch of space was filled with storage racks in which all the stock was displayed in categories and alphabetically. The walls were plastered with posters. With its thrumming music and laidback vibe, there was a hint of teenage bedroom about it.

Sometimes Reece wondered whether he'd refused to grow up. It wasn't for lack of academic ability that he hadn't been able to pursue a professional career which would've paid more money. It's just that he'd have always felt as if he'd sold out. A square peg in a round hole. That's how he'd felt as a teenager growing up. Not alone, he guessed, to feel that way. To want to kick back against the rules of traditional education.

During the summer, the large window to the street caught the sun. As the mercury rose, the shop interior could become unbearably hot. To counteract this, the entrance door was always wedged open.

It was through the doorway that the detective and his sidekick appeared unannounced, reminding Reece of that unsettling time after Ashleigh's death when his life had been turned upside down. The lines between private and public became blurry. Coming so soon after the death of Helen, the whole time had been crushing. He had lost his wife and stepdaughter within a year.

'Should I have been expecting you?' asked Reece, instantly regretting that his words sounded defensive. That's what a murder investigation does to you, he thought. It makes you trip over yourself.

'We were just passing,' said DI Jack Sheppard. 'Wanted to show Stanley where you work. Just to help give him a bit of context.'

Reece noticed the private investigator taking in his surroundings. Was he looking for something? 'I expect you're thinking the name is unfortunate?' said Reece. '*Criminal Records.*'

'Is there a demand for vinyl records these days?' asked Stanley, side-stepping the question. 'I thought it was all about streaming now?'

It was a common misconception. 'You'd be surprised. What once looked like a thing of the past has bounced back into fashion. There's been a resurgence of people wanting to hold something *real*. The experience of listening to a record appeals to lots of people.'

'So it's not just DJs,' Stanley observed.

'No. Not at all. And it's not collectors either. It's much broader than that. Almost a kick back against the idea of digital.'

Reece sensed a disinterest from Jack Sheppard whilst Stanley appeared to show a genuine desire to hear more.

'These aren't just artists from yesteryear,' said Stanley, starting to rifle through the covers.

'Absolutely not. There's a strong market for contemporary

artists. Their fans want to own a piece of their work. It's not just the small independent labels bucking the trend. The big players want a piece of the action too.'

'You run this place alone?' asked Stanley.

'That's right,' said Reece. 'Started it as a labour of love, really. It's never actually felt like work.'

'But no other staff? You don't find it lonely?'

Reece wondered whether Stanley was talking from personal experience.

'It doesn't really warrant another pair of hands. I'd find it tough to cover the cost of that too. And in answer to your question about whether it's lonely, no. There's always someone popping in, and there's a true sense of community with the other traders on this street.'

Stanley looked to understand. If he wasn't mistaken, his eyes had grown a little misty.

'Can you tell us,' said Jack abruptly, 'do you have any reason to believe that Ashleigh might've been pregnant at the time of her death?'

'Pregnant?' Of all the things that had occurred to him, this hadn't been one of them. 'What makes you think that?'

The air felt thick. Reece wondered whether he detected a tension between the two men. As if, perhaps, they weren't entirely on the same page.

'It's a potential line of inquiry that might've been overlooked,' said Jack.

Reece shook his head. 'I was worried about this type of thing.' He looked at Stanley who he felt might be the more understanding of the two. He wasn't sure why. Just something in his demeanour. Something softer than his counterpart.

'Worried?' asked Stanley.

'When Helen died, I worried that I wouldn't be able to fulfil that role for Ashleigh. The role of mother, I mean. Daughters need their mother, don't they? There are things that aren't so easy to discuss if it's not with a mother.'

Reece didn't know if he'd expressed himself clearly. He

hadn't shared his concerns before. Although, Stanley looked to be sympathetic to his feelings.

'It can't have been easy,' said Stanley.

'No. I hadn't considered what things would be like if Helen wasn't around. You don't, do you? I mean, you can't spend your life worrying about things that might never happen.'

'But it did,' said Stanley, in a tone that sounded like he understood.

Reece nodded. 'During Helen's illness, it felt as if we were a family. It didn't matter to me that Ashleigh wasn't my birth daughter. To me, she *was* my daughter. It was only when Helen died that things changed somehow. I don't think Ashleigh felt comfortable with the thought of living with her step-father. As if the bond we had only existed because of her mother.'

'Is that why she took the job as a live-in nanny, do you think?'

'I told her that she was welcome to stay with me. It was her family home.'

'But you couldn't make her change her mind.'

'I didn't want her to move in with the Rainsfords. I really didn't.'

Reece spoke the truth. Although, if truth really be told, there was more than one reason why he hadn't wanted her to live with them.

Jack didn't like to admit that he could be slow on the uptake when it came to other people's feelings. But even he would be hard pushed not to pick up on Stanley's silence on leaving *Criminal Records*.

'What's the matter?' he said. 'Cat got your tongue?'

'We hadn't agreed to ask Reece about the possible pregnancy. I thought we might've sat on that information for a while, just to see how we felt about it.'

'Oh, come on,' said Jack. 'I wasn't going to let a chance go by to gauge his reaction.'

They came to a halt at a pedestrian crossing. As they waited for the lights to change, Jack asked, 'Where next?'

'There are some things I want to follow-up having looked at the case files.'

'Great,' said Jack eagerly. 'Where to first?'

The lights changed from green to red and the traffic stopped. The pair crossed the road. On reaching the opposite pavement, Stanley said, 'You go on. This time I'll pursue this on my own.'

And before he'd had a chance to answer, Stanley was off. Alone.

CHAPTER 12

Stanley didn't look back over his shoulder. He wouldn't. He refused to give Jack any satisfaction at noting a second glance.

His progress, however, was suddenly impeded by an unforeseen crocodile of foreign exchange students speaking loudly at one another in another language. It wasn't Italian. He'd have grasped a little of their conversations if it had been. His steps drew to a halt as they filed around him, a mass of clipboards and backpacks.

He hoped that Jack hadn't lingered to witness the scene.

Stanley tried to push his frustrations from his mind. It had always been the danger in accepting the job; that his personal experience would mar his judgement. He was drawing a conclusion that when it came to Jack Sheppard, you were either on one side of his fence or the other. In his camp, or not.

The last of the student stragglers passed and Stanley's progress continued.

A short distance along the road, almost directly opposite *Criminal Records*, Stanley walked into the perfumed interior of a hair salon.

'Can I help you?' asked a woman at a wooden counter. She, like the place itself, looked to have been trapped in a time-warp. Her slightly-too-dark-to-be-natural hair was piled high on her head in a glamorous beehive.

'I hope you might,' said Stanley.

The whir of a colleague blow-drying a client's hair provided an opportunity to speak more discreetly, although he sensed he was being watched in the mirrors.

He pulled out his contact card which she took with

manicured ruby fingers. She reached for her reading glasses. Her eyes were drawn with thick black liner.

'A private investigator?' she said.

'Yes.' He imagined that the seats provided fruitful gossip and hearsay on local comings and goings. But that wasn't exactly what he was here for. 'I'm working with the police to review the case of a young woman who was murdered.'

'That'll be Ashleigh James,' said the woman. 'A terrible thing. Such a tragedy with all her life ahead of her. You know her step-father owns the shop over the road?'

'I do.'

'We're a nice little community here,' she said. 'We like to look out for one another. Being an independent retailer isn't easy. Not in this economic climate. It's important to support each other.'

Stanley approved of the sentiment. Although, what this support might've looked like he wasn't sure. Besides, it wasn't the angle he'd come to pursue. 'I believe that all the retailers on this street were approached by officers, asking whether you'd noticed anything unusual on the day Ashleigh's body was discovered?'

'That's right,' she said. 'They said it was just standard procedure. We assumed that they had ear-marked Reece as a suspect and were trying to check up on his movements that day.'

'I saw in the case files that you hadn't seen anything of note.'

'It was just another ordinary day. Hot, from what I remember.'

'So nothing unusual?'

'No,' she said. 'Funny, but when someone asks you to recall details of a day it's unnerving how little of the details you can remember. Unless something out of the ordinary happens, it all rolls into a bit of a blur.'

'I noticed in the files that the police also appealed for any CCTV footage from key locations.'

Stanley followed her line of sight as she turned her coiffed head towards a small camera installed on the corner of the ceiling. It pointed across the interior of the shop and out through the window. There was a high chance that its scope would include the frontage of *Criminal Records*.

'Everything gets recorded on to a computer,' she said vaguely. 'New technology. I don't really know how it all works. I explained that to the officers. Said I'd have to ask my grandson to check whether any footage was available from that day.'

'And did you?'

'I did. Gary – that's my grandson – said that he could still access the footage.'

Stanley knew that the case files showed no record of this information. 'But there was never any follow-up from the police, was there?'

She shook her head. 'No. They never came back. To be honest, I sort of forgot about it. I thought that it couldn't really have been that important if they didn't come back.'

'And do you still have the footage?'

She exuded a quiet exasperation. 'I don't know. I would have to ask Gary again.'

For his next port of call, Stanley phoned ahead. Best, he thought, to check what time would be convenient.

At the agreed time, he approached the entrance. It was a converted period house. In its day it would've been called a villa. It sat at the western end of the promenade looking back across the beaches of Clifton Sands. Through the tall sash windows, he heard the sound of children's voices. The unfiltered energy of youth.

Stanley recalled that the nursery was attached to a private school. This looked to be evident in the slick branding that emblazoned the entrance.

As he buzzed the intercom, he thought how much had changed since his own childhood. The notion of security and safeguarding of young people had hardly existed. His memories of playing in the street were unrestrained by subsequent concerns regarding health and safety.

At being greeted at the door by the nursery manager, Stanley hoped he concealed his surprise at her being so young.

'Stanley Messina?' she said. 'I'm Fran.'

The same branding from the front of the building was stitched on an emerald green polo shirt.

'Thanks for making the time to see me,' said Stanley.

'Not a problem,' she said, breezily. 'Although I'm not sure if I'll be able to add much to what you already know.'

Fran had a natural professional air about her. It was immediately clear that she was suited to her role. Anyone would feel confident to leave their child in her care. To find a vocation that sat well with one's character was all you could ask for, Stanley thought.

They walked together as Fran explained that the nursery catered for pre-school children. Some people, she said, were surprised at how young some of the babies they looked after were. A consequence of working parents feeling the pressure to return to jobs as soon as possible. Her tone was matter of fact. No hint of judgement.

'The routines are important,' she said. 'That's what we're good at.'

To send a child here couldn't be cheap, Stanley thought. Being linked to a prestigious school made him wonder whether this might be a foot in the door, the first rung on a career ladder. It made him want to shudder. He didn't like to think that life might not be a level-playing field, a race in which some were privileged to a head start.

Fran led them into a neat functional office. 'Please, take a seat.'

'I told you on the phone that I'm helping review the Ashleigh James case,' said Stanley.

'I still find it hard to believe. That something like that could happen here in Clifton Sands. To someone we knew.' Her words sounded sincere. 'She was such a kind girl. A real natural.'

'A natural? You mean in terms of childcare?'

'Exactly. It's not always the way, I'm afraid. I suppose though, in Ashleigh's case, she'd been looking after her mother for some time. So perhaps that had formed her in some way.'

Stanley pulled out his little notebook and flicked through his own notes. 'She joined you straight after her final year at school?'

'Yes. It's usual for placements to be secured whilst they're still at school. We work with the college to organise their training. Not that she completed any qualifications with us in the end though.'

'No?'

'You don't need any formal qualifications to work as a nanny.'

'And did you have an opinion on Ashleigh going to work for the Rainsfords?'

'I was disappointed to lose her. She worked hard and, as I said, she was brilliant with the children. It was losing her mother, I think. That's what really made her mind up. She wanted to be independent.' This echoed a version of what Reece had conveyed. 'Although, I'm not sure that's quite how it worked out for her. Not from what we heard.'

Stanley wanted to know more. 'What did you hear? From whom?'

'Just bits and pieces, really. Tittle tattle. Bernadette used to fill us in.'

'They came to work here together after school I understand.'

'Not unusual to have trainees from the same school. But I can't say that we'd ever had two girls who'd been such close friends. Hard to describe really. The type of friendship that can only really happen as teenagers. If that makes sense?' She looked slightly preoccupied. The way in which she studied the empty floor suggested possible thoughts that had never occurred to her before. 'Bernadette would tell us that Ashleigh was struggling with the workload at the Rainsfords. That what they expected from her was unreasonable.' This mirrored what Stanley had already heard. 'She had a boyfriend too, I believe.'

Stanley gave her a moment to reflect on her own words.

'It sounds like her desire for independence came at a cost,' Stanley observed.

'That's just what I was thinking.'

'During the time she worked here with you, can you think of any reason why anyone would want to harm her?'

'Oh no,' said Fran. 'Not at all. That's what makes it all so shocking. She was good natured and likeable. Always the first to take others under her wing. It makes it all the worse in some ways. That bad things can happen to good people.'

Stanley agreed.

They talked through some of the finer details regarding dates and timelines, of which everything seemed to tally. Fran said that she would think more about it but was pretty certain there'd be nothing else that might be helpful. She was sorry not to have shed more light on things.

On heading back towards the front door, securely sealed from the outside world, Stanley observed through an inner window the girls and boys at play. A small group had gathered around a table of building blocks. An argument appeared to have sparked. Podgy little hands were grasping at one another, hitting out with staccato punches. Before an adult had a chance to intervene one girl had grabbed another by her hair and was tugging violently. The scream brought a swift intervention from another branded t-shirt.

'Children can be so cruel,' said Fran. 'But bet your hat that all will be forgotten in five minutes.'

Could the same, Stanley wondered, be said of grown-ups?

It didn't feel right on such a beautiful day to be thinking of murder.

Stanley walked the promenade towards town. The sea sparkled. A light aeroplane buzzed lazily along the horizon.

He looked out across the beaches and the stick figures that

populated them. It had been a day like this, he supposed. People had been enjoying themselves in the summer heat, basking in the sunshine. Ice creams had been licked. Ball games played.

Yet whilst the crowds enjoyed their seaside leisure, the horror at the Rainsford's summerhouse was playing out. Ashleigh struck by a single blow. She'd slumped to the ground.

And still the gentle waves lapped onto the pebbles. The soft splash of water folding. The epitome of a bucket and spade summer.

Her bitter end.

The gulls still laughing.

CHAPTER 13

As a teenager, Jacinta had been an avid reader of romance novels. She hadn't cared that others had thought them cheap and trashy, or that each book followed a well-trodden formula. For her, they represented a possibility that life might hold more for her than the beige suburbia in which she'd grown up.

Why can't I focus? She asked herself.

This room, which had once been a bedroom, was set up as a personal pilates and yoga space. She laid out a mat and worked through a variety of poses.

Usually, she'd achieve a clear mind by concentrating on her breathing. Being aware of air filling her lungs before escaping through her nose.

Today, however, her thoughts flitted about like a nest of grasshoppers. She was thinking of the books she used to devour. The stories that were guaranteed a happy ending. Of being rescued from the mundane by a wealthy prince or dashing billionaire. Who wouldn't want that?

She stood and stretched before transitioning into warrior pose.

Had she been duped by those stories? Those tales that had never gone further than passionate embraces. Never to explore what happily ever after actually looked like. Of getting to know one another intimately. To become bored with one another. To see each other growing old. Those things lay beyond the final pages of any book.

The window was slightly ajar. Through it, Jacinta heard Sophie and Bernadette playing games.

She hoped that her daughter might see the world differently.

Not pin her identity on the apparent power of a man. But instead to be confident in her own ability to forge a rewarding path. To find happiness with an equal.

She changed pose again, pushing her limbs to their limits.

Lately, Jacinta had wondered whether Sophie was growing up in a bubble. In achieving her own dream, her daughter existed in a limited sphere of privilege. What impact, if any, would this have on her outlook on life? What parent wouldn't want to provide the best for their child?

Again, such things had never occurred to the heroines in those novels. Never had they encountered a corpse in their garden. Not a single one of them.

After her yoga session, which had done little to ease her scattered thoughts, Jacinta took a shower. She hoped that the hot water upon her skin might relax her. The bathroom, one of several at the house, was decorated luxuriously. The decadent fixtures and fittings were the best money could buy, with the handmade tiles being imported from Morocco.

She turned off the taps and dabbed herself with a fluffy towel. Her spa-like surroundings, despite being familiar, had an alien air to them. In the steamy mirror, her reflection bounced back at her like an actress.

Imposter syndrome? She wondered. How sad to feel like that after all these years. To harbour a niggling doubt at the back of her mind that perhaps she wasn't worthy of this comfortable life. That it hadn't been achieved through her own merits.

At some point in time – she couldn't say when – it had occurred to her that it could all be snatched away.

It was probably the envelopes. That's what had triggered this feeling, alerting her to a growing sense that she'd tried to ignore. Even that he kept such things from her signalled a shift in how she felt about their relationship. Not that it should have come as any great surprise. How much did she really know about his business? Hadn't he always assumed that she wouldn't be interested, or not understand?

She'd found them by accident. In the simple, and innocent, act of hunting for a pen to write a shopping list. They'd been stuffed into one of his study drawers.

What it was about their appearance that piqued her interest, she couldn't say. Nothing but simple curiosity.

She'd looked at the contents in mild horror. Her eyes scanned the pages trying to fathom what she was looking at.

Some wives may have confronted their husbands about it. But instead, she had furtively returned them to the their hiding place and hoped that he wouldn't notice that they'd been disturbed.

Having blow-dried her hair, Jacinta sat at her dressing table and pulled a brush through the knotty strands. She tugged in long strokes, making her scalp sting. The window looked out on to the terraced garden and to the steep downs beyond. They kept that gate locked now. Before, they'd never thought twice about leaving it open. Not once had she believed that the terrible things you saw on the news could penetrate the boundaries of their comfortable existence.

How naïve she'd been. Her outlook the consequence of all those romance novels she'd read.

She'd always trusted Oliver to do the right thing. For her, and for Sophie. She'd built him up in her head as their protector; the romantic hero. Seeing what she chose to see in him.

Hadn't he always encouraged her to pursue her dreams? Never wanting to clip her wings.

And so she had responded in kind, enabling him to continue living a life unshackled by domestic chores or restrictive family life. Confident, all that time, that the love they had for one another remained, whether together or apart. Wasn't Sophie proof of this? The living embodiment of their connection.

She clutched the hairbrush to her chest and felt her heart beating.

Trust is taken for granted, she thought. It's something not thought about until you do. And once you begin to think about it, you wonder how it ever could've been so effortless before.

In the garden, a game of chase was underway. Jacinta gazed at a miniature version of herself clambering up the steps, giggling in delight as her pursuer danced after her on light feet. Shouldn't she be happy at their special little bond? Wasn't it good to see her daughter happy? That's why they'd employed a nanny.

They were on the grass now, picking daisies to make chains. To see them playing so close to the decrepit summerhouse made her shudder. She drew near to the windowpane, unintentionally catching the young woman's attention, whose face turned expressionless in her direction.

Jacinta drew back with a start.

From downstairs, she heard him coming in through the front door. She looked at her watch. It was the usual time he returned.

'Hello!' he called. 'Is anybody home?'

'Daddy! I want Daddy!'

Oliver heard Sophie's wails rising from downstairs. Bernadette was trying, unsuccessfully, to placate her.

'He's got important business to do,' she was saying. 'He'll play with us as soon as he can.'

He softly shut the study door. He'd said his Hello to Jacinta. Her cool kiss upon his cheek still lingered. They would update each other on the day's events later over a meal and a glass of wine.

More than once, Jacinta had said: 'The company is your other woman, isn't she?'

She'd been joking, of course. Making light of the torn loyalties that so frequently removed him from family life. Better, he thought, than being accused of having a roving eye.

Whether she liked it or not, Oliver had always felt a weight of responsibility as the man of the house. Just as he occupied the position of chief at *Progressive Pathways*, so too did he stand as head of the family. Not a modern way of looking at things, granted. But, in his eyes, it was not about roles or discussions of equality. It was about control. Being in charge. Keeping things in order.

His phone pinged again.

In days gone by, he wouldn't have thought about switching it off. There'd been no line at which the business stopped and his own life began. The two were inherently interlaced. One and the same thing.

It was Ashleigh who had confronted him on it. As much for her own sake as his.

Owning a business, he'd explained, didn't conform to convenient nine to five hours. Success, he insisted, required constant attention; *obsession* even.

'That doesn't help the rest of us,' she'd snapped. 'Not knowing where the lines lie. Disrupting any routine for Sophie.'

He hadn't reacted well to her criticism, pointing his finger angrily with accusations of playing Mary Poppins. With hindsight, he regretted his tone. He wasn't used to being challenged. Having his own daughter used as emotional collateral had side-swiped him.

And, secretly, he'd admired her for standing up to him. Her feistiness had been unexpectedly attractive.

The phone pinged once more.

It was probably the damned accountant again, bombarding him with more spreadsheets and red ink numbers. Impressing on him the severity of the situation. Indirectly forcing him to make decisions following their recent conversations. What was it he'd said about maintaining the status quo simply not being an option?

Oliver considered his surroundings. The quiet neatness of the study stood in stark contrast to the humming force of London. Here, there was little to separate domestic life and career. Only, in fact, a wooden door.

He thought again of Ashleigh. Of how she'd expressed similar concerns for herself.

She'd been holding a glass of wine. Her vacant eyes suggested she wasn't a drinker. He'd been guilty of forgetting how young she was.

'It's like I'm in a cage,' she'd said, her speech a little slurry. 'A very comfortable cage that I don't know whether I want to be in or not.'

'That's called a *gilded* cage,' he'd said, probably sounding rather pompous as he explained the concept.

'That sounds about right,' she'd agreed. 'Living here is like a dream. I mean, look at it! It's luxury. But am I really happy? Do I have freedom?'

He'd challenged her as to whether any adult has freedom. The conversation now felt particularly pertinent. He recalled how charged the air had felt in that low-lit kitchen. Jacinta had been flying, Sophie tucked up in bed.

He gripped the edge of the desk, trying to quell a silent foreboding. The walls appeared to be closing in on him, his world in danger of shrinking.

It wasn't how he'd felt in the past. The business had always been about growth. In building it up, his own sense of self had expanded alongside the revenue and profits. The trajectory had always been ascending.

Weren't there theories about how the universe was slowly imploding? He thought of black holes in deep space, shrinking back to nothingness.

It made him wonder if it were true of his own life, on a smaller scale. Had there been a moment – unnoticed at the time – when things had switched from forward to reverse. Those around him would probably point towards the corpse of a young woman discovered in his garden. An obvious point in which his life had fractured.

But that was only what had been seen.

He glanced at where he'd once put those envelopes in his desk drawers. They'd started arriving soon after Ashleigh moved in. A stark reminder that, although past actions may be invisible, they aren't necessarily gone forever.

'You can leave at any time,' he'd said to Ashleigh. Testing her? Flirtatiously? 'The door to the cage is open.'

And she had skulled the remnants of her glass before gently stumbling away to her room, with Oliver wondering whether he should follow or not...

CHAPTER 14

The terrain behind the Rainsford's house was sloped. It marked, Jack explained to Stanley, the edge of the South Downs way; an area of natural beauty popular with ramblers and tourists. On the parched grass, well-trodden tracks zig-zagged out in numerous directions.

Jack panted as they ascended the slope. Stanley, he noted, didn't seem to be as out of breath as him. Despite his chinos and shirt with rolled up sleeves, he hadn't even broken a sweat. Whilst Jack, on the other hand, in a pair of football shorts could feel his face reddening in the heat.

'Watch your step,' warned Jack. 'Adders like to bask in the heat. They come out of the long grass.'

Stanley, apparently unperturbed, mumbled something to himself.

'What did you say?' asked Jack.

'Vulnerable,' said Stanley. 'I was thinking that a person on their own could be vulnerable walking here. It's surprisingly remote considering how close it is to the town.'

'But there's no evidence to suggest that Ashleigh was walking here that day. She was in the back garden of the house.'

'And you say that there were no reports of anything unusual before then? No prowlers or suspicious activities?'

'Nothing,' said Jack.

'It helps to see how the house sits in its surroundings.' Stanley nodded at the chimney stacks peeking out above the wild shrubs and twisted trees. 'Makes you realise how private the place is. It raises questions.'

'Yes?' Jack wheezed. He was in danger of getting a stitch.

'We don't know for certain that Ashleigh's killer entered the property through the rear gate. But *if* they did, was it because they were familiar with this entrance? Had they visited the house that way before? Or was it because they wanted to creep in? To avoid being seen at the front entrance?'

'What we *do* know is that there was no suggestion of any struggle. Which points towards the killer being someone that Ashleigh knew.'

'It's just whether this person was expected by her or not. Are you okay? Do you need to stop for a bit?'

Jack held his sides. 'Not sure when I got so unfit.'

They took a moment. Beyond the twittering of native birds, the low soundscape of a British seaside resort on a summer's day washed over them.

'From everything I've gleaned so far,' said Stanley, 'Ashleigh's world grew smaller when she became the Rainsford's nanny. She lived in quite a small sphere. That fateful afternoon, she had been granted some precious free time by her employers. On a rare day together, Jacinta and Oliver had taken Sophie to the beach. Based on what she was wearing, it seems fair to say that Ahsleigh hadn't intended to go out. There was a book beside her in the summerhouse?'

'Yes. A romance novel. Not something very heavy.'

'So who does that leave? Maybe she'd invited a friend to visit. Bernadette?'

'She said she was at home that afternoon. Her parents vouched for her.'

'Then a boyfriend, perhaps?'

'The Rainsfords didn't like him coming to the house.'

'Are we clear on why?' asked Stanley.

'Seems pretty obvious to me why not,' said Jack.

'And besides,' Stanley added, 'Ashleigh may have chosen to defy her employers by inviting Lorenzo to the house regardless. Where did he say he was that afternoon?'

'He was driving his car up and down the seafront. Part of the boyracer brigade, I suppose.'

'A little old for that?'

'Exactly. There were reports of him driving erratically. Showing off, no doubt.'

'Which only leaves her step-father. Where was Reece that afternoon?'

'In the shop.'

Jack wasn't sure where the conversation had got them. It reminded him of the frustrating briefings in the incident room, during which it had felt as if they'd been going round in circles.

'The alibis for all of them are very flimsy,' said Stanley. 'As are any potential motives.'

'Any theories on that front?' asked Jack.

'A few.'

Jack waited.

When no further words came, he said: 'Care to share?'

'All in good time.'

They set off again on one of the tracks that skirted the rear boundaries of the houses and gardens on the Rainsford's road. This time, however, Stanley seemed to have set a slower pace for his companion. Jack didn't like to think of himself as someone requiring slowing down for. It made him feel grumpy.

'There was *something* I forgot to ask you about,' said Stanley.

'Oh?' Jack grunted.

'You said something about a locket belonging to Ashleigh? I looked in the case files. It was only mentioned tentatively that it might be missing.'

'It's an example of us being under-resourced. The team was spread too thin, being pulled in competing directions. We couldn't be sure whether it held any significance because the recording of evidence hadn't been as tight as it might've been.'

Jack realised how easily he'd shared this perspective with Stanley. It wasn't the type of thing he'd say to just anyone.

'Can you try and explain?' asked Stanley. 'I'm not sure I

understand.'

'It didn't come to light until sometime after Ashleigh's death. From memory, it was Reece who asked when her personal belongings might be released, and who they would be given to. He mentioned that Ashleigh always wore a locket on a chain around her neck. It had a photo of her Mum in it. But there was no record of her having been wearing it when she was discovered. Neither was it found in any of her possessions in her bedroom at the house.'

'And you didn't think it was of particular significance?'

'As I say, I couldn't be sure that the team had accounted for everything. We only really had Reece's say so that she always wore it.'

They had reached the gate now. It was sturdy and tall with a curved top edge, and sat within a brick arch. Thistles and nettles were evidence now that it was no longer used. The wildness of the land around them suddenly sat in stark contrast to the manicured environment obstructed by the wooden gate. Two entirely different worlds.

'Seen enough?' asked Jack.

Stanley nodded. 'Seeing things in person always puts a different complexion on things.'

They sat in Jack's parked car with the windows down. Having reviewed their progress thus far, their focus now turned to what the next steps would be.

'We haven't spoken to Oliver yet,' said Stanley.

'Jacinta made it pretty clear that she didn't want us at the house.'

'She did. So it's a good job that her work takes her away from home. I've looked at her regular flying routes and there's a fair chance that she'll be off again tomorrow. And Oliver looks like he might be around.'

'He's pretty elusive,' said Jack. 'Filthy rich, too.'

'Does that bother you?'

Jack grunted. 'Fair play to him. It looks like he's made it

through hard work.'

Stanley didn't reply. He looked to be thinking. Jack was coming to understand that in such moments, Stanley Messina could be distant. It was like an invisible forcefield around him.

Jack felt ashamed that he couldn't remember whether this had always been the case. The circumstances under which they'd met had determined their first interactions. There'd been an obvious imbalance of power. Little wonder, when you thought about it, why the man today might've grown wary and guarded.

I'd just been doing my job, Jack thought. The evidence had been black and white. Or so they'd thought.

'What's brought you to Clifton Sands?' he asked.

Stanley wasn't quick to answer. In danger of overstepping the mark, Jack supposed.

Eventually, as if he chose his words wisely, Stanley said: 'I needed a change. A clean break.'

'A fresh start?'

'Something like that.'

Jack could see the merits of that, although he wasn't convinced it was the whole story. Closing his eyes and randomly putting a pin into a map didn't seem like Stanley's style. From what he'd seen, Stanley never did anything by chance. His approach was pragmatic and reasoned. The qualities that Jack had thought necessary to review this case.

'You don't like to talk about yourself, do you?' said Jack.

'I'd rather stick to business. Keeps it less complicated.'

Jack decided not to push it. What did it matter to him if Stanley wanted to be private? It was hardly as if he was prone to gushing emotions and feelings himself, was it? And yet, there was a part of him that wanted to warn Stanley against being completely closed off to the world. He wouldn't want to think that's what they'd done to him.

Who would he be to talk anyway? People in glass houses and all that...

He looked at his watch. Kick off would be on the TV soon.

'Fancy watching the match at mine?' he asked.

'No thank you.'

Jack shrugged and turned the key in the ignition. 'Suit yourself.'

Sylvia Smith drank too much.

Whether this was the reason she'd resorted to renting her spare room, Stanley couldn't say for certain. All he knew for sure was that her breath usually smelt of alcohol and she furtively disposed of countless glass bottles.

Her two-bedroom flat was on one of the grimy backstreets where gulls scavenged on litter and sirens frequently roared by. Located on the first floor up a communal flight of stairs, the interior was an eclectic mix of Sylvia's exotic tastes. She had a penchant for leopard print and lurid paintings of faraway places.

'I don't allow smoking inside,' she'd said when showing him the room. 'You'll have to smoke on the doorstep like me.'

Hearing that he didn't smoke appeared to surprise her. Different, he guessed, from the usual paying guests.

Beyond the broken capillaries and bloodshot eyes, Stanley sensed a kind soul. Not someone to be underestimated, though. Her hair, dyed and scooped up with a tortoiseshell clip, suggested a bohemian history.

'Whatever's happened in your past is your business,' she'd said, knowing that such an arrangement might attract lodgers with dubious backgrounds. 'I don't judge. Everyone has a story. All I ask is that the month's rent is paid upfront in cash.'

Stanley guessed that the money would never be declared, the bank notes passing undetected from the tax office's grasp.

He'd agreed on the spot.

And Sylvia hadn't raised a pencilled eyebrow at his lack of belongings. For any man of his age to have only one suitcase would, for most, raise suspicion. A clear indicator that unfortunate events had come before.

This evening, Stanley sat on the lumpy bed mulling over the

investigation. Through the bedroom door, dramatic voices from a soap opera drifted. Sylvia, he'd noticed, had to raise the volume to hear. On heavy nights, she would slump with a glass still in her hand. Hypocritical, he'd thought, to pity her for being alone.

He hadn't liked Jack asking questions. He hadn't liked how it had made him feel.

It hadn't always been this way. There'd been a past version of himself who'd have welcomed conversations. But who could blame him? To speak would only be to risk showing his true self. To make connections would risk getting hurt.

He was thinking of Ashleigh now as much as himself.

It was the word *vulnerable* again.

She had taken risks to start a new life for herself. And look where that had got her.

Death.

The room was gloomy. Had he simply replaced one set of walls with four more, he wondered. Could he escape the confines of this self-imposed existence? Would he even want to?

He reached out slowly and pulled the handle on the bedside table. It was just where he'd left it. The silver teeth on the key glinted in the half-light. It made him think of Pandora's box. He considered lifting it, to know that it was real, before thinking better of it. Instead, opting to slide the drawer back into its casing. Hidden again from view.

CHAPTER 15

The smoke from Lorenzo's cigarette caught in the breeze as he scuttled over the wooden planks. Through the gaps between them he could see the rusted legs of the pier disappearing into the swirling water beneath.

It was, as he'd hoped, too early for tourists. The place was all but deserted. That's why he'd suggested it. The perfect venue for just such an assignation.

Strange, he thought, how the place he'd once walked hand in hand with her could feel so different now. It had glistened and shone back then. Nothing like the rundown structure that confronted him now. Even the sea had lost its sparkle, churning now in a dirty brown stew.

He placed his hand upon his pocket, just to check that what he'd slipped inside was still there.

And it was.

Reaching the isolated furthest point at which the railings overlooked the waves, a figure stood where they'd agreed to meet. Lorenzo had arrived slightly late in the hope that he'd already be there.

'Stanley Messina,' said Lorenzo to the man who'd come to the restaurant with Detective Inspector Jack Sheppard. 'You came.'

Stanley nodded. 'I said I would.'

Lorenzo had phoned him. He told him he'd prefer to speak in person.

'I don't really know where to begin,' he said, flicking the glowing nub of his cigarette over the edge. The private investigator had sharp inquisitive eyes, but they didn't look like those of the police.

'Take your time. Maybe start with what prompted you to ask me here today…'

Yes, Lorenzo thought. That would be a good place to start: 'It was Ashleigh's step-father, Reece. He called me to say that you'd paid him a visit with that detective, who'd said that Ashleigh might've be pregnant. He wanted to know if that was true.'

'And was it?'

'If it was, she never mentioned it to me.'

'But it could've been?'

'We were always careful. She wasn't on the pill as it didn't agree with her. So I took, well you know…'

'Precautions.'

It wasn't a word that Lorenzo would've used. 'I guess nothing's one hundred percent reliable though, is it. It shook me up a little bit, to be honest. To think that I might've been a father. Why would Jack Sheppard tell Reece something like that, and not me?'

Stanley didn't answer.

The breeze from the water blew a little more aggressively. There was a chill to it.

'That's what the whole investigation was like,' said Lorenzo. 'We were played off against one another. All of us treated as if we were guilty. Me, especially. And it made us all close ranks. Made us suspicious of each other. That's why Reece called me, I guess. He wanted to know whether I'd been keeping things from him.'

'How would you say you got on with Reece?'

'I only met him a handful of times before Ashleigh died. He was still cut up about Ashleigh's mum dying. He said he just wanted the best for Ashleigh. He asked me to look out for her.'

'What do you think he meant by that?'

'He wasn't sure about her working for the Rainsfords. He never thought it was a good idea. He'd rather she'd have stayed at home. I guess we've both wondered whether we did enough. Maybe it was worse for him...'

'Worse? In what way?'

'Well, I think he felt that not only had he let Ashleigh down, but he'd let her mother down too. He'd failed on the promise to keep Ashleigh safe.'

'Do you think he's being fair on himself?'

'No,' said Lorenzo. 'Not at all. Ashleigh was incredibly headstrong and determined. She knew her own mind and nothing would stop her from doing what she wanted to do.'

The waves beneath them slapped against the iron girders. Lorenzo thought how distant the promenade appeared. The hotel facades looked like toy town. It was a place he felt both entirely embroiled and simultaneously alien.

'You haven't told me how you and Ashleigh met,' said Stanley.

'It was purely by chance. Ashleigh was still working at that posh nursery then. She was out one day with a child when one of the wheels on the pushchair came loose. I just happened to be passing. I'm good with mechanics, so was able to help her fix the wheel back on. We just sort of got talking. It was like we clicked. I asked her whether she'd like to meet up some time. And it just went from there.'

Stanley looked to be genuinely interested. 'Sometimes love can strike when we least expect it. Would you say that you were in love?'

As they had got to know one another, Lorenzo had found himself thinking about Ashleigh all the time. He stored up things in his head that he thought she'd like to know and look forward to hearing what she'd been up to. He'd never felt that way about a woman before; needing to be close to her, to protect her.

'I loved her, yes.'

'And do you think she felt the same way?'

Stanley Messina wasn't afraid of asking the difficult questions.

'She said she did. She joked that I was her prince in a

fairytale. At first, I liked that. It sounded romantic. Until she said that she was like a princess locked in a tower.'

'Was she referring to her situation with the Rainsfords?'

'Oliver Rainsford wouldn't let me visit Ashleigh at the house. He told her that he didn't want strangers there. She'd said that I wasn't a stranger, but he'd still refused. It was a weird set up, her living and working there. He thought it gave him the right to dictate what she could and couldn't do. Men like him think they have power.'

'Men like him?'

'Yeah. Men with money. They think they're better than men like me, don't they?'

The temperature of his bones began to rise. Stanley must've observed a change in him, as he asked: 'Are you okay?'

'If only she'd *listened* to me. I told her that house wasn't a place she wanted to be in. It was messing with her head not knowing where work ended and life began. She said that she had to think about the little girl. Sometimes it seemed as if she was almost her mother. It looked completely messed up to me.'

'Was there anything specific you saw that concerned you?'

'No,' said Lorenzo. 'It was more of a *feeling*. The way Ashleigh described being controlled. It made me think that she wasn't safe there.'

'Did you tell the police that?'

The heat rose again. It threatened to move from a simmer to boiling. 'Do you think that detective wanted to listen to anything I had to say? Okay, I hold my hands up. I haven't always been well behaved in the past. When I was younger I got in with the wrong crowd. Got into some fights, that type of thing. I got known to the police with a few convictions. That was all the police could see. It was like they weren't going to accept that I'd turned my life around.'

Was Lorenzo imagining it, or was Stanley blinking back tears?

'The investigation could've been handled differently,' said Stanley, sounding as if he wasn't necessarily referring to the case in hand.

'It was like they'd decided I was guilty and their job was to try and find anything that could pin Ashleigh's death on me.'

'Exactly,' Stanley agreed.

'You believe me, don't you? You believe I didn't kill her?'

'I've no reason to believe you are lying to me.'

'I won't lie to you.'

'Then tell me this, why were there reports of you driving erratically on the seafront on the day Ashleigh was killed?'

'The detective told you that?'

'No. It was in the case files I'm reviewing.'

'It'll sound weird, but meeting Ashleigh made me look at my life differently. She made me want to be a better person. I think, too, seeing her question her own career made me think about what was important to me too. To hear her talk about the boundaries of work and life made me wonder whether I should make some changes. I've always worked in the family restaurant, you see. It's sort of just been expected. An unspoken agreement. That's not where my passion lies though. Being a mechanic is what I want to do. That day I'd plucked up courage to tell my parents that I didn't want to work at the restaurant anymore. It was too much trying to do that and work at the garage.'

'The conversation didn't go well?'

Lorenzo recalled the raised voices. The accusations of being ungrateful, disloyal, lazy. It had quickly escalated to barbed comments of him being a disappointment.

'I was angry. It was the side of me that I didn't want Ashleigh to see. The side that she made me want to fight against. So I let off steam by being in the car alone.'

'Being with Ashleigh made you think about your own future.'

'That's right. It was sort of like before her I was stuck in some kind of strange box. In meeting her, doors started to appear. Doors to things and places I'd never known existed. She made me feel that I had other possibilities. Opportunities. That's the type of person Ashleigh was.'

'I would like to have met her,' said Stanley.

'Do you think there's a chance of finding her killer? If all those police officers couldn't, how will you?'

'There were, as you say, a lot of people working on the case. That, perhaps, was the problem. Too many strands being followed – or not followed up properly – as we might yet find. Too many chances for things to slip between the cracks.'

It certainly sounded as if Stanley Messina might approach things differently. His demeanour, from the way he dressed to the way he spoke, wasn't the same as that detective, Jack Sheppard. An arrogant sort. Going at things like a bull at a gate. The type who let power go to his head.

'Funny line of work,' said Lorenzo, 'being a private investigator. Have you always been one?'

'No,' Stanley replied. 'I was like you. With the doors, I mean.'

'When one door closes another one opens. Isn't that what they say?'

Stanley didn't answer immediately. He'd clenched his hands together and now wrung them thoughtfully. 'For me, a door closed and I spent so long looking at it that I didn't even realise there was another door. Let alone that it was open.'

Lorenzo wasn't sure he understood. Too cryptic. Although, there was something in the way he spoke that felt comfortable. Something trustworthy and open.

'Messina? Is that an Italian name?'

'Yes,' said Stanley. 'My family are from Sicily.'

Although wanting to ask more, Lorenzo didn't want to overstep the mark. It was enough to know that he might understand something of being an outsider too.

'I want to see justice for Ashleigh,' said Lorenzo.

'That's what I want as well. That's what I do my job for.'

Lorenzo believed him.

He slid his hand into his pocket. It was a risk. To share this with Stanley Messina, or not. He could only go with gut instinct. The man seemed genuine.

The wind whipped up again. This time it was wet and salty like tears.

'I have something to show you,' said Lorenzo.

'Yes?'

His hand encased the cold object in his trouser pocket. He pulled out his closed fist before uncurling his fingers to reveal what lay within…

CHAPTER 16

In addition to Jacinta's white Porsche, Oliver kept two other cars in their double garage. One was a fuel-guzzling four-wheel drive beast, the other a slick fully electric saloon.

It was useful to have them both, providing a choice as to how he could present himself in different situations. The electric car was all well and good for his eco credentials, but hardly intimidating.

This morning he'd pulled them both out on the driveway. Jacinta never understood why he chose to wash them himself.

'Can't you pay someone to do that?' she'd say.

It was her answer to most things. Nearly everything could be solved with money.

Having sprayed the soapy suds away with a jet of water, Oliver turned off the hose at the tap. However much success he'd achieved, he still remained frugal. A shared trait, apparently, in many an entrepreneur. Never being able to shake the memory of starting out with nothing. Watching the pennies so that the pounds might look after themselves.

And besides, cleaning the car gave him another reason to get out of the house. As much as he loved his young daughter dearly, there were only so many games he could play with Sophie.

He was just reaching for the chamois leather when the two men sauntered on to the driveway. The detective was instantly familiar to him, although not his companion. Jacinta had said they'd be wanting to talk with him.

They looked a little too comfortable with their surroundings for Oliver's liking.

'Gentlemen,' he said. 'How can I help you?'

'I expect Jacinta told you that we are reviewing the investigation of Ashleigh's case,' said DI Jack Sheppard. Oliver remembered him as a bolshy type. Nothing about his manner today made him change his opinion.

'She did. She said you'd probably call again, but that she doesn't want Sophie to be around.'

'And is she?'

'She's playing in the garden with Bernadette. So we can talk freely here for now.'

'This is Stanley Messina. A private investigator. He's looking at the case as an impartial third party.'

Oliver wondered what credentials such an investigator might hold. How would it look if he questioned whether he was qualified for the task at hand?

He realised that he was squeezing the chamois so hard that his knuckles had turned white.

'If I may just confirm your whereabouts on the day that Ashleigh was murdered,' said Stanley. 'You were on the beach with Jacinta and Sophie?'

'Yes. We had a family day.'

'So you were each other's alibis?'

'The beach was crowded. There were plenty of people who could have vouched for us if anyone had cared to follow up.'

Jack Sheppard looked about to speak only to think better of it and let Stanley Messina continue.

'Was there anything you noticed about Ashleigh's behaviour prior to her murder that might've seemed different or out of character?'

Oliver's experience of making presentations at work stood him in good stead. Appearances, he'd learnt, were so very important.

'As I told the police at the time, she was often quiet and withdrawn. It hadn't been long since her mother died. She was processing that, I think. We felt the police wanted to accuse us of working Ashleigh too hard. I'd even go so far as saying they thought we locked her up. But that just wasn't the case. It was her choice to spend so much time here. We tried to encourage her to go out. Do things that young people do.'

'So there were no incidents that happened that drew your attention?'

'Incidents?'

'Possible arguments? Confrontations? Strange behaviour?'

'No,' he said. And how easy the lie slipped from his lips. His heart pumped a little faster. He must retain his game face. 'We've shared everything we could with the police. I don't know what else we can do to assist. On that afternoon, our lives were turned upside down. A cliché, I know. But it's true. An *evil* entered our home that day. A killer who is still out there roaming around. Can you imagine what that's been like to live with? Day in, day out.'

'Things that are unresolved can be the most difficult to cope with,' said Stanley. 'That's why it's so important to unlock the truth...'

'Too early for the pub, I guess?'

Stanley was starting to get used to Jack's persistent pull to the nearest watering hole. He didn't know whether this had started since retirement or if – very likely – it had been a part of his working life. How different, Stanley thought, working for the police must be. To always be on the right side of things. Part of the comforting and reassuring system. A system that many never question, until it fails them.

Working alone had its challenges, Stanley found. Managing his workload, organising finance, having to fathom out problems on his own. It was frequently a challenge. Although, through all the challenges he could resolutely be himself.

Could that be said of those within institutions such as the police? He wondered. What compromises would someone have to make to clamber up the greasy pole in that special club? What parts of yourself would you have to give up to fit in?

'It's too early for me,' said Stanley. 'And I'm on paid time. Time that *you're* paying for, remember?'

'Doesn't that entitle me to a say as to where we hold review meetings?'

'No,' said Stanley. 'You're paying for my independent investigative services. There's no hierarchy here. No position of authority or power.'

Jack swung the car under the height barrier of an open-air public town centre car park

'So what did you glean from meeting Mr Rainsford?' asked Jack, turning off the engine.

'I sensed a man who likes to be in control. The type who conducts their home life much as they do they work life – businesslike.'

'Anything in that, do you think, which might help your review?'

'I don't know,' said Stanley. 'My mind was running through an idea that perhaps Oliver has created his own little universe. I'm thinking of his business and his homes. Everything exactly how *he* wants them to be.'

'Sort of like he's playing at being God?'

'I'm not sure. But just suppose he's used to getting his own way. Could he treat those in the circle he's created as things he has the right to tell what to do?'

'That fits with the suggestion that Ashleigh might've been struggling with her rights as a live-in employee.'

Stanley noticed two seagulls on one of the lampposts. They were pecking at one another. Aggressively or affectionately, Stanley didn't know.

His mind was travailing two lines of thought. What was it that he'd been thinking about Jack and the police force? He rewound his brain, feeling that somehow it might be relevant.

He made a stab at putting it into words: 'If you're inside a world that's been carefully constructed – either through chance or design – I suppose there's a danger that you might lose touch with the wider world. Only seeing what's going on through the lens of that small existence.'

'Like being brainwashed?'

'I was thinking more of being *institutionalised*.'

'Hmm.'

If Jack had felt the word being thrown at him too, he hadn't immediately shown it. What it meant that he didn't look to think that it might've applied to him, Stanley wasn't sure. An indication, perhaps, that he might still be in that world of the police force, if only now in his head. Not easy, after all those years, to give up a position of power. To feel confident about calling the shots.

Jack moved on: 'What else?'

'I was running through some *what ifs*...'

'Always a good game,' said Jack, flippantly. To Stanley, it was no game.

'There's no evidence to support it, so we'd have to treat the idea very cautiously, but what if there had been something between Ashleigh and Oliver.'

'An affair, you mean?'

It didn't fit with Lorenzo's version of how things were. He'd insisted that they'd been strong. There'd even been talk of love.

'Let's not take anything off the table. An affair, maybe. Something coercive, possibly. Either way, is there a chance that Ashleigh could've been carrying Oliver's child?'

'If we're considering every possible situation, then there's a chance. Which would give motives to others. How would Lorenzo have reacted if he'd found out?'

Stanley noted how quick Jack was to point the finger at Lorenzo again. 'Oliver himself might've reacted badly. How would he be sure that the child was his? Or just suppose Jacinta was aware of the situation? Where would that leave her?'

Jack didn't look to be listening. He was squinting as if trying to draw imaginary lines to identify potential links between all the possible suspects. 'Why hadn't I thought of that before?' he said to himself. 'Oliver's love of cars. Could there be a link there to Lorenzo, a mechanic at a local garage?'

The link, Stanley thought, was tenuous and might be tinged with Jack's prejudice towards Lorenzo.

'Maybe.' said Stanley. 'Or…'

'Or what?'

'What if your observation about the cars is too literal.'

'Nope, you've lost me there.'

'Did you notice that Oliver's cars were brand new?'

'That's 'cos he can afford them.'

'Yes. But what if it demonstrates something of his character? A trait that could be applied to other areas of his life. Just say, for example, he has a history of trading in old for new…'

'Ah,' said Jack. 'Now you're talking. What if he'd once traded in an older model for Jacinta? Might that show that he's got form. That he could've done the same with Ashleigh? A leopard and his spots and all that…'

'It's a giant leap,' said Stanley, instantly worried that they might be in danger of tracking in the wrong direction.

'Worth exploring though,' Jack replied. 'Leave it to me…'

Oliver tore along the coastal road. He needed to be out of the house, to try and clear his head.

The route along the cliff-tops was well-known for slow moving traffic. In addition to the day-trippers taking in the view of downlands and the English Channel, there were open top buses and ice cream vans.

Oliver accelerated hard and swerved around each obstacle. A near miss with an oncoming motorbike set his heart pounding, adrenalin buzzing through his body.

He had no destination in mind. He just wanted to drive.

The feeling in the pit of his stomach grew. It was guilt, he supposed. That's what it did to you. It slowly overcame you – consuming you, and everything around you, entirely. It became heavier and heavier. An invisible burden to be carried hour after hour, day after day.

He felt physically sick. He considered pulling over and retching at the roadside, but instead opened the window to let in fresh air. It blasted his face.

Was it just guilt? He wondered. Or was it the fear of being found out? Of being publicly humiliated. Disgraced.

It had been done. And things done in the past are out of reach.

Oliver let out a cry and smacked his hand on the steering wheel. If only he could go back, rewind time to the moment before he made that decision. It would spare him this terrible place of despair – a place he was locked in mentally with no means of escape. Just like an escapologist, he was in a box being lowered into a river. The water rose. He was up to his neck in it now. And soon he would be going under.

If only he could go back and change events.

If only he could change what happened.

If only….

If only…

CHAPTER 17

Sometimes the shop was busy. On such occasions, Reece would nudge up the volume and savour the customers browsing the racks of vinyl records, pulling them out to marvel at the artwork on their covers. The buzz of such moments, Reece thought, transcended the trudging banality of everyday life. To see *Criminal Records* thriving dispersed the curse of what other people might think.

Helen had always encouraged him and the business. 'Life's too short to be following other people's dreams,' she'd say. 'You've got to do *you*.' He'd never liked to question her too hard, but her husband's – Ashleigh's father – tragic accident had shaped her outlook. Life, she understood, was fragile. And time was something that should never be taken for granted.

Of course, the shop wasn't always thrumming with custom. Retail, Reece had learnt, was an ever ebb and flow of activity, frequently unpredictable in its nature. Such was the case this afternoon. After a slow flow of regulars in the morning, the afternoon trade had petered out.

He usually saw these quieter times as an opportunity to source more stock online. He'd cross-check the records for sale with his elaborate database to ensure that all were listed and stored in the most appropriate category. Sometimes – if he could face it – he'd even have a look at the accounts.

From his position behind the counter, he watched the mishmash of people passing by the shop window. If the sensational headlines of the national tabloids were to be believed, Clifton Sands was nothing more than a seaside town in decline. Even its once quaint reputation as a favoured retirement destination was coming under threat, with tales of county lines gangs and drug-dealing grannies roaming the streets of boarded up houses. The truth, however, from Reece's direct vantage point, looked to be much more complex. The people who walked by were of all ages and backgrounds, a rich tapestry of various nationalities, classes and gender. Its very nature as a tourist destination brought diversity. Not something that sat well with everyone. Reece'd seen the angry comments on social media discussion groups berating the town for not being what it once had, for losing its charm. He didn't scroll through them too long. It depressed him. Some people, he reasoned, would never like change.

If life had taught him anything over the last couple of difficult years, it was that change happened whether you liked it or not. He thought of meeting Helen and the optimistic glow that had embodied and all the things they'd talked about doing together. He recalled learning of Helen's daughter and the mix of emotions at unexpectedly becoming a stepfather to Ashleigh. The memories came flooding back. They crashed down upon him, intruding on the present. Sometimes he wondered whether he'd been punished for being smug at having been so happy at a family life he'd never imagined would happen. Helen's diagnosis had changed everything. The universe had laughed at Reece's delight at finding happiness. From that point on, everything had teetered upon what seemed like a frozen lake on which hair-line fractures began to spread out across its surface.

It remained a terrible contradiction in his head that Helen's deterioration had been agonisingly slow to witness whilst also losing her so quickly. He likened it to watching a terrible accident, like a car crash or collapsing building. Seeing a horror unfurl within seconds but experiencing in something like slow motion.

Little wonder, he supposed, that some people didn't like change.

When Ashleigh had come into his life, he'd been surprised at her youth. He'd always thought he'd remained young at heart, resolutely – in his own mind at least – refusing to grow up. There'd always been something of the teenage boy about *Criminal Records*. And yet, with Ashleigh's arrival he'd been struck by how old he appeared in her eyes. The way in which she saw the world was unfathomably different from his. It had, he was ashamed to admit, unsettled him at first. It made him look back at his own teenage years and wonder at how or where the intervening time had gone.

She'd thought that's why he hadn't wanted her to work for the Rainsfords. It was her opinion that Reece thought that being a nanny wasn't good enough for her, that she wasn't fulfilling her potential. In one of her fiercer moments, she'd even accused him of being jealous that time was still on her side. After what she had gone through with her mother's illness, she said she'd deserved some time to work out what her future might look like.

He hadn't liked that they'd argued. It made him ashamed of what Helen would've thought. And besides, what she'd accused him of just wasn't true. Yes, for some people the old adage about their schooldays being their happiest was true. But not for Reece. Looking at the complexities of being a teenager through the lens of time passed, going back to that age filled him with terror.

What use would thinking about it all again do? It was that detective and private investigator, swirling everything up like mud from the bottom of a pond.

It was because of them, he supposed, that he turned his attention to the file on his computer labelled 'Finance'. Whilst the accounting side of the business had always been a chore, Reece understood its importance and his ordered brain had never shied away from keeping things up to date. He recorded income and expenses meticulously.

He had wondered at the time whether they might've looked at his accounts. Perhaps they had? Can't the police do that type of thing remotely? Probably not without your permission, he thought.

He wasn't sure how he'd have been able to explain it. Such a large anonymous deposit.

I deserved it, Reece told himself. After all I'd been through, I deserved it. Not to have to worry about how the next bill would get paid, never to have to queue at the foodbank again...

Jacinta stood before the full-length mirror in their luxurious bedroom. She wore nothing but her underwear.

She often scrutinised her own physique, obsessing over a perceived lack of tautness or a dimple on her skin that she hadn't seen before. However hard she tried to keep herself in shape, the effect of age and gravity was a battle she feared she couldn't win.

A pinch of her flesh at the waist made her despair at the lack of elasticity. Why didn't her skin spring back as quickly as it once had? It felt squidgy like putty.

No wonder Oliver hasn't been near me physically, she thought.

Lately, he'd seemed more distracted than usual. Sometimes she'd caught him gazing off into space, entirely caught up in his own silent thoughts and unaware of his surroundings.

Jacinta wondered whether he was thinking of Ashleigh. Some days she lingered about the place like a ghost. Never would Ashleigh have to worry about getting lines on her face or cellulite on her thighs. Her youth would be preserved forever. How could anyone compete with that?

She thought again of the detective, Jack Sheppard. His lack of response to any kind of flirting niggled at her. Most men were simple to handle in that respect. And yet, he remained entirely impervious to her charms.

It wouldn't do. No, in order to see her plan through she'd need to find another way forward. She had faced obstacles in life before, so this was nothing new. It would just require some lateral thinking.

Seizing upon a sudden new line of possibility, she grabbed her phone from the dressing table and accessed the internet. The screen lit up her face. It always amazed her that so much information could be held in something as small as the palm of her hand. Everything you might ever need to know – and things you didn't – hidden within like an Aladdin's cave.

She opened a search engine and began to type. She'd remembered his name, probably because it was unusual. Her thumbs spelt it out.

Stanley Messina.

She hit search.

What was she expecting to find? She didn't know.

A stream of headlines on numerous news outlets sprang up. She brought her face closer to the screen. Was this him? The same man?

She opened up a photo to look more closely. He was standing on steps outside an official building, surrounded by journalists and photographers. He looked pale and a little thinner, but there was no doubt that it was him.

It made a lot of sense. Probably the reason for him doing his current occupation.

Suddenly, she felt a little dizzy.

There was a prick of her conscience. Was somebody going to get hurt if she followed through with her plan? Too late now, she thought. The wheels were already in motion. What she'd already done would have consequences. It was a web in which somebody would get trapped, just – so it transpired – as Stanley Messina had once been in the past.

Lorenzo would've liked to have gone to the gym more. He'd heard people talk of their *happy place*. And whilst not going so far as that, it was certainly a place that he could be himself. He enjoyed the unspoken camaraderie between the other people who trained there. It made him feel connected. Almost part of a community.

Unlike other people who struggled with motivation to attend

regularly, Lorenzo's restriction on visiting the gym was time. With work at the garage and his persistent ties to the family restaurant, Saturday and Sunday mornings were usually all he could spare. These were peak times, of course, so the place was usually thrumming with activity. The cardio equipment – treadmills, rowing machines and exercise bikes – whirred at full pelt. Red-faced, sweaty clients clustered around the resistance machines and jostled for the free weights. Dance music with a heavy bassline thudded from the wall-mounted speakers.

Entering the gym through its sliding doors, Lorenzo always felt the outside world slipping away. Inside this buzzing cocoon, his mind could focus on the here and now. Not be concerned about what had happened in the past or what might happen in the future. He'd put his trust in Stanley Messina. There was nothing to be done now. Just wait, and hope, that the private investigator would come good for him.

Lorenzo made his way to his favourite corner of the gym where punchbags hung from the ceiling. It was where he liked to burn off his aggression, to assuage the Latin fire in his blood. He'd pummel with his fists until he was out of breath and sweat escaped from him in huge droplets.

This morning, as he pulled on his gloves in preparation to box, he froze. Across the terrain of the hot gym interior, he was taken aback at the sight of her. What had brought her here? He'd never seen her here before.

She looked around her inquisitively as if searching for something in particular.

Their history was awkward, to say the least.

He shuffled on his feet like a fighter in the ring. He didn't like the feeling of the outside penetrating his safe space.

His hopes that she might not see him were shattered as her face turned in his direction. At first, they looked at one another impassively, waiting it seemed for one to signal to the other. Then, with a flashed wave she skirted her way across the floor towards him.

'Lorenzo,' she said, 'I thought it was you.'

'Yes,' he replied, somewhat pointlessly. It was clear who he was. 'They've given you the day off?' he said. His tone implied more than the obvious.

'Sophie's with her parents today,' said Bernadette.

Lorenzo wasn't sure how to feel. Being with her brought back too many memories. They were crowding in at the back of his mind.

'I haven't seen you here before,' he said. 'You train here?'

'Oh no,' she replied, pausing for a second as if for emphasis. 'I'm here for the self-defence classes…'

CHAPTER 18

In the garden of the bungalow, Stanley discovered two deck chairs positioned in the shade of a particularly flowery parasol.

'Beer?' asked Jack through the window to the crazy-paved patio.

'No,' said Stanley.

'There's one of those poncy Italian lagers in the fridge, if you want one.'

That was no accident, thought Stanley. But that was no reason to slip into bad habits. Just because someone had taken the time to think of him.

'No, I'm fine. Honestly.' Adding: 'But thank you anyway,' to soften the blow. 'I'll have a water, please?'

'It'll only be from the tap. Haven't got any fancy sparkling stuff.'

Stanley said that tap water would be just fine.

'Ok,' Jack's voice called back from inside.

Whilst the lawn looked to have been recently mowed, Stanley noticed that the borders were tumbling with overgrown shrubs and wildflowers looked to have self-sown from the nearby downs. There were some pots with brown stalks within them, evidence of perhaps bedding plants in the past. The roses that he'd seen in the front garden too looked not to have been dead headed.

'I'm not very green-fingered,' said Jack, stepping out with a glass of water in one hand and a brown bottle in the other. 'I like keeping the grass tidy. Using a lawn mower clears the head. The rest of it's beyond me though. God knows what she'd make of it.'

The glass of water was thrust in Stanley's direction. Jack looked particularly bulky dressed in his shorts, football shirt and sandals. His arms and legs were thick and hairy.

'Did the bungalow belong to your mother?' asked Stanley, having already thought this might be the case.

'Uh-huh,' said Jack. 'It still does.'

Stanley thought he understood. 'She's unwell?'

Jack plonked himself heavily into the deckchair. It sagged and groaned under his weight. 'She got old,' he said, gruffly. 'What with my retirement and everything, I thought it'd be easier to put my stuff in storage and rent out my flat. Save me driving back and forth all the time. A sense of duty, or something. I don't know.'

Odd, Stanley thought, to think of any parallels between them. Impossible to deny, however, that they'd both been separated from their possessions. Liberated even, perhaps.

'It doesn't sound easy,' said Stanley, assuming that Jack's mother might be in a nursing home. It went some way to explain the hushed phone calls.

'Mum's being well looked after.' Jack swigged his beer. 'Besides, what is it they say? People only move to Clifton Sands to die?'

Stanley hoped it was just black humour.

In contrast, it suddenly struck him how alive their surroundings were. The encroaching wildness upon what had once been a manicured garden buzzed with insects. Two butterflies fluttered chaotically in haphazard flight.

Not for the first time, Stanley feared that his paid time might be more for companionship than reaching justice for Ashleigh James.

Before he had a chance to focus their attention back to the investigation, Jack abruptly continued to talk about themselves.

'Are you not lonely?' he asked. 'You seem to spend a lot of time alone.'

'No,' said Stanley.

'You had a partner, didn't you. Before it all happened.'

Stanley felt his defences rising. 'I'm not sure what this has to do with the case…'

'Do you not want to talk about it because of who I am?' asked Jack. 'Or do you blame me for it all?'

Stanley had a good mind to walk away. This wasn't what he'd signed up for. Not to feel like he was – once again – on the wrong side of Jack's bully boy interrogation techniques.

Jack bulldozed on: 'It's funny, but I spent all those years in the police having to be strong. Putting a brave face on everything. Avoiding talking about emotions and feelings. I thought it was a way of supporting everyone else. Keeping the team happy. And yet, now that I've left the force, I wonder if I got it wrong. Who I was on the outside wasn't the same as the person I was on the inside. Does that sound weird?'

Stanley shook his head. 'It doesn't sound weird.'

'Look, to be blunt,' said Jack, 'I feel bad about everything that happened. I know I was just doing my job, following the evidence and everything. I *am* sorry.'

'You were only doing your job. It wasn't your fault.'

Jack leant forward in his deck chair. 'You mean that? You *really* mean that?'

'Yes,' said Stanley. 'I do.'

There seemed to be almost a physical release in Jack's demeanour as if an actual weight had been lifted from his shoulders. As if, perhaps, this is what he'd hoped for.

'You don't know what that means to me,' said Jack, although Stanley felt sure that he did.

To have one's name cleared could be the most important thing in the world. It could change everything.

'On good days,' Stanley said, 'I can rationalise that it was all just an unfortunate set of events. A terrible coming together of unconnected things, that snowballed with no particular malice.'

'And on bad days?'

'On bad days I think about everything I had and wonder if

any of it was real at all.'

Jack sucked air through his teeth. 'That's heavy, mate.' He looked into the neck of his bottle. The following extended silence Stanley didn't know whether to attribute to an awkwardness or a reflection on his own working life; years, Stanley suspected, Jack had begun to question.

Stanley didn't know how to feel about an unlikely bond forming. The Jack Sheppard in his head was the embodiment of everything he despised. And yet, here in the sunlight, he began to wonder whether he'd been guilty of prejudice. Perhaps choosing to hold onto a simple version of the man in order to have someone to berate in his mind's eye. It had been a way of coping, he supposed. Trying to make sense of it.

The word that had hung about this whole business re-emerged in Stanley's mind.

Vulnerable.

He didn't like it. He wanted to swot it away like one of the insects buzzing about the garden.

What was he afraid of? Afraid that opening up would unleash a torrent of feelings and emotions? Or that sharing his past – his self – would leave him open to the pain of being hurt again?

If he wasn't so deep now in this case, Stanley would've thought of walking away. But he had to admit that the mystery of Ashleigh's death had gotten under his skin. She deserved a better outcome than simply a file stamped 'unsolved'. His dogged determination, a trait that had ultimately pulled him through the worst of trials in the past, couldn't let it go now.

'Shall we get back to business,' said Stanley.

Jack looked happy to move back on to safer ground. 'Yes. Let's review our progress.'

Stanley didn't have much to report. He'd been working through the whereabouts of the suspects as outlined in the case files on the day of Ashleigh's murder, the recordings of which had been haphazard. And yet nothing unexplainable had leapt out at him.

There was, of course, the matter of his rendezvous with Lorenzo at the end of the pier. What he'd shared with him had set his thoughts moving in ways he hadn't considered before. However, with a nagging sense that Jack had always had Lorenzo's card marked, he decided not to tell him of their meeting at this point. To be keeping secrets didn't reflect well on their working relationship, Stanley thought.

'Any more thoughts on the possibility of Ashleigh being pregnant?' asked Jack.

'I've been keeping that in mind as I've been reviewing the evidence. As far as I can see, it's something we could only really take Bernadette's word for.'

The distinct lack of progress on Stanley's behalf seemed not to bother Jack at all. And not for the first time Stanley wondered whether instead Jack was grateful that things mightn't be tied up too quickly. For all their gruff interactions with one another, Jack clearly appreciated the company.

'Well,' said Jack, 'I've been doing a bit of digging myself.'

'Yes?'

'You remember we talked about looking more into back stories? To see if there might've been something we'd overlooked?'

'That's right. Have you found something?'

'I have,' said Jack. 'But I don't know whether it's significant.'

Stanley leaned in to hear more as Jack reached down and picked up a manilla folder.

Jack continued: 'The internet's a bit of a rabbit warren, isn't it? Amazingly illuminating if you know what you're searching for though. I started looking at the website of *Progressive Pathways*. That's Oliver Rainsford's business, you'll remember.'

'I do,' said Stanley. 'Careers advice and guidance.'

'Exactly. A sort of one-stop shop for everything in regards to career development and employment opportunities. It's a very slick and sophisticated set up with Oliver very much front and centre of the brand. There's a section on the website about his own experience. His qualifications got him to Oxford University.'

'So living proof of the value of education.'

'Indeed.'

So far, so normal, thought Stanley. Only the manner in which Jack was stretching out the tale suggested that some revelation might lie ahead.

'It was from there, as I said, that I started digging. His CV was listed on a business networking site so I was able to cross-reference his education and work dates to see if they were legitimate. Yes, I know. A suspicious mind. But everything tallied. It was on his CV, however, that I saw that he'd attended a secondary school in Clifton Sands, which got me wondering...'

'Which school?'

'Oliver got a scholarship to attend *Manor School*, one of the most prestigious and expensive schools in the country.'

It was the very school that the nursery Ashleigh had worked at was attached to.

Jack began to rifle through scraps of paper in his folder. 'Where did I put it? I know it's in here somewhere.' It was another glimpse into how his cases had been run in the past. 'Ah, here it is...'

Stanley waited.

'Those kind of places always have networks, don't they?' said Jack. 'That's what they pride themselves on. Showing off the successes and heritage of their past students. It didn't take me long to find various groups and pages on social media with old boys sharing their memories, reminiscing about the good old days.'

Good old school days. It wasn't the first time that had been said in this investigation, Stanley recalled.

'It's called death scrolling,' Jack continued. 'You start scrolling down through post after post, photo after photo. That's what I was doing. Not knowing what I might be looking for. Until eventually I found this...'

At last, the sheet of paper in his hand was held out for Stanley to see.

On it was a grainy photo.

'The quality's not great, sorry,' said Jack. 'My printer's old.'

Stanley peered at the image, not entirely sure what he was looking at. There were several rows of figures lined up in various heights. All dressed uniformly in matching school ties and blazers. They looked to be young men rather than boys.

'It's the upper sixth form in the year that Oliver attended Manor School,' Jack said. One of his classmates had posted it. Jack pointed at one of the faces. 'Recognise him?'

Stanley looked closer. Beneath centre-parted hair, the features were obvious. 'Oliver,' said Stanley. 'He looks like he's laughing or larking about?'

'That's what I thought. Him and the fellow next to him. They look like they're a couple of jokers…'

Stanley sensed that he was missing something.

Jack was enjoying his moment. 'Why don't you look again?'

'Nope. I can't see anything.'

'The young man next to Oliver. The one he's sharing a joke with. They're obviously close. They even look alike. But look beneath his friend's floppy hair…

'Oh! Is that…?'

Stanley looked to Jack for confirmation but was halted by the vibrating buzz of his phone. He took the call then solemnly hung up.

'What is it?' Jack asked. 'Who was that?'

'It's Bernadette,' he replied. 'She's been attacked…'

CHAPTER 19

'I can't go like this,' said Jack, looking down at his shorts and football shirt. 'Give me a moment to get changed.'

Stanley waited on the doorstep of the bungalow. His thoughts were occupied with the information that Jack had shared. He wondered at its significance. This development with Bernadette troubled him too. Did it mark an escalation in their investigation? Had they stirred up the hornets' nest? It was a terrible cliché. But it was the simplest way of looking at things.

Jack emerged from the front door in a pair of black jeans and a crumpled T shirt. On seeing Stanley's reaction, he said: 'It's all I had that was clean.'

'I'll drive,' said Stanley, thinking of the beer.

Jack looked ready to protest but then apparently thought better of it and opened the passenger door to the car.

Pulling away, Stanley sensed a frisson of excitement from Jack. The thrill of the chase, he supposed. His career in the police force had probably seen him thrive on adrenalin-fuelled incidents. The buzz of them had likely been addictive.

'What are you thinking?' asked Jack, almost panting.

'I'm keeping an open mind,' said Stanley calmly. 'And I'm processing the information you just shared with me.'

'The photo?'

'Yes,' said Stanley. 'It was Reece James stood beside Oliver Rainsford, wasn't it?'

'Uh-huh. Looks like they were at school together.'

Stanley considered this as he navigated their way through the roads across town. 'There was no mention of this during your whole investigation?'

'No,' said Jack. 'We're talking about going back decades. Why would either of them have mentioned it?'

It was the hidden connection that troubled Stanley. A reminder that the things under the surface would probably lead to Ashleigh's killer.

'Do you think Oliver knew that Reece was Ashleigh's stepfather?' asked Jack.

'I don't know.'

'Or did Reece know who Ashleigh was going to work for? I've never got the feeling that Reece thought particularly highly of the Rainsfords.'

Stanley tried to recall the conversations they'd had with both men. What new complexion did this extra information put on what they'd said?

Jack continued: 'I read somewhere once that friendships never last more than seven years. There's some kind of cycle in which they reach the end of their usefulness.'

It was a harsh assessment and Stanley wondered whether he spoke from personal experience.

'You make it sound like changing socks,' said Stanley.

'Friendships can be complicated, can't they?'

A random thought flickered through Stanley's brain. Easier, perhaps to pinpoint where many friendships ended than when they had once begun. He was thinking more of himself than the case at hand.

'Do you think it's different for men?' asked Jack. 'You know, friendships and all that?'

As if proving the point, Stanley felt himself retreating from the conversation, concerned that they were in danger of straying away from the investigation. What use would there be in having a heart to heart? They travelled onwards in a strange companionable silence. Always they seemed to be traversing an unspoken divide.

Stanley parked on the wide road where the Rainsfords imposing house was located.

They were greeted by an ashen faced Jacinta, who stood looking thin at the open front door. She had the air of a gatekeeper.

'I wanted to phone the police,' she said, pointedly focusing her attention on Stanley rather than Jack. 'But Bernadette said that she had contacted you, that she wanted to see you first.'

'What happened?' Stanley asked, stepping over the threshold.

Jacinta looked distracted. 'I've put Sophie in front of the TV. I'm hoping that will hold her attention. Oliver's not home. It was Bernadette's day off. She went out and did her own thing.' Stanley thought of the day that Ashleigh had died. It had been her day off too. 'She came through the front door with blood on her face. My first thought was to make sure that Sophie didn't see.'

It showed where her priorities lay.

'What had happened?' Stanley asked again having not had a sufficient answer.

'She was crying. Almost inconsolable. She said that she'd been walking back here when someone had crept up on her and pushed her over. She'd caught her head on the brick pavement. There was a nasty cut on her forehead and blood was pouring out.'

Stanley recalled a case from the past in which such a head injury had been fatal.

'Did she see who it was that pushed her?' asked Stanley.

Jacinta shook her head. 'I couldn't get a word from her. She was pretty shaken up. Would you like to go up and see her? She's expecting you.'

There came an awkward moment when it was unclear as to whether the invitation was being extended to both men. Stanley sensed Jack bristling beside him at the prospect of being excluded.

'It's okay,' said Jack. 'You go.'

Climbing the staircase alone, he looked back at Jack and Jacinta stood wordlessly beside one another. There was history there, but Stanley felt that Jacinta's air was somehow different from their first encounter. The sight of blood, it seemed, had shocked her. Hadn't it been she who had found Ashleigh's body? It made him wonder what feelings and memories Bernadette's appearance had brought back to her.

The door to her bedroom – which had once been Ashleigh's – was ajar. It struck him how many overlapping threads there were between these people. Things upon things.

He gave a little knock.

'Hello?' she said.

'Bernadette. It's me. Stanley.'

He nudged the door open to reveal her perched on the edge of the bed. Her hair was bedraggled and her eyes red and puffy. On her forehead was a large fabric plaster that was stained a dark red.

'Am I okay to come in?' he asked.

'Yes,' she said.

'Can you tell me what happened?'

'It all happened in a flash. There's not much to tell.'

'Okay, let's just go take it step by step. Jacinta said it's your day off?'

'Yes,' said Bernadette. 'I needed to go into town to pick up some things. You know, toiletries and stuff. Nothing exciting. The weather was fine, so I walked instead of catching the bus.'

Stanley moved further into the room. 'May I?' he asked, gesturing at the space beside her on the bed.

'Of course,' she replied, shuffling a little over to make space for him.

'Tell me, did you notice anything unusual when you were running your errands in town?'

'Unusual? In what way?'

'Were you aware of anyone following you, for example?'

Bernadette looked vaguely into the middle-distance as if trying to conjure up memories in her mind's eye. She squinted a little and flinched, raising her hand up to her bandaged forehead.

'I think it's shaken me a little,' she said. 'I can't really remember much. It'll sound weird but I feel like I've been looking over my shoulder recently. As if there's a shadow following me…'

She looked and sounded vulnerable. It was that word again.

'Can you remember when that feeling started?' Stanley asked.

Bernadette peered again into the empty space before her, shaking her head. 'Somewhere between now and forever,' she croaked.

It was an obscure answer.

'Where exactly were you when this happened?' asked Stanley.

'I was almost back here at the house.' Stanley noted that she didn't use the word 'home'. 'The road was quiet. There was nobody about. Suddenly, somebody pushed me from behind.'

'You hadn't heard them approach?'

'No,' she said. 'Perhaps they were hiding? Waiting for me?'

'Can you think of anyone who would do that?'

Her eyes brimmed heavily with tears. 'I just keep thinking of Ashleigh. It's just like that, isn't it? You know, like what happened to her?'

'Were any of your belongings taken?' Stanley asked.

Bernadette scanned her immediate surroundings as if the thought hadn't occurred to her. 'I don't think so. No, I had a bag with my purse and shopping in it. I was still carrying that when I got back here.'

'Have you any reason to believe that somebody wishes you any harm?'

'No,' she sniffed. 'No, I really don't. It's just…'

'Go on…'

'It's just, I can't help thinking about Ashleigh. As if I've almost stepped into her shoes somehow. And I know it sounds silly, but I worry that I'm in danger just because I'm *here*. Just my being here.'

Stanley thought back to the time they'd met in the park.

She'd asked him then if he could guarantee her safety. When had that been now? Somewhere between now and forever…

Once again, he didn't feel in a position to promise to protect her.

The sound of a cartoon playing on the TV in the neighbouring room drifted uneasily out to them. Its frantic jolliness was at odds with the obvious tension in the house.

Jack felt rudderless as he looked up to where Stanley and Bernadette were in private conversation.

'Is this what you wanted?' Jacinta asked, her arms tightly folded.

'Sorry?'

'Were you hoping to rake everything up with this *re-investigation* of yours? Didn't you think you'd made enough of a mess of it all the first-time round? Thought you'd come back to have a second crack at it?'

'Well, listen here. I know you were never much of a fan of mine but…'

'A fan? You came into our lives and treated us all as if we were criminals. Innocent until proven guilty, they say. But not in your case. Not with Detective Inspector Jack Sheppard. Only content until you'd tried to drag all our names through the mud.'

'Now that's not…'

'Fair? Don't talk to me about what's fair. We've had to cope with the constant ongoing spotlight of media attention because of your incompetence. Your inability to get a case solved. And still it goes on. If we tell the police that Bernadette has been attacked, the hacks will be back, peddling their stories for the world to pick over.'

Jack knew he was a sitting duck. His pride wouldn't let him step away.

'I want justice for Ashleigh,' he said.

'Rubbish. This is about your ego. It's about you trying to salvage your reputation. Look at you. You're pathetic. What are you without the trappings of the police force around you? Things were starting to get better for us. But you've brought those things back into our life again.'

'Things? What things?'

'Oh, I don't know. Bad things. People, I suppose.'

'Who?' asked Jack. 'Who has come back into your lives?'

Jacinta leaned in and with lowered voice said, 'Ashleigh's boyfriend for one.'

'Lorenzo Conti?'

'That's him. He was always trouble, wasn't he.'

The hunch Jack had harboured during the initial investigation returned. 'Has he been hanging around?'

'Sniffing around Bernadette, I understand. It's almost as if history is repeating itself, wouldn't you say?'

Classic Auto Repairs didn't trade on weekends. Lorenzo's boss, however, never minded him tinkering alone. He'd put on a playlist and either work on one of their long-term projects or just have a general tidy up.

Today, he was in the pit, stretching up to the rusty underside of a vintage Alfa Romeo. He tried to focus his attention on his assessment of the vehicle, only to find his thoughts tracking back to Ashleigh.

It was seeing Bernadette at the gym. How she felt the need to take self-defence classes. He recalled how Ashleigh had described uncertainty about Oliver, to which Lorenzo had reacted strongly, accusing him of being a sleaze. He'd demanded to know whether Oliver had overstepped the boundaries as her employer. And he'd seen her clam up. He'd regretted being so hot headed.

He shone a light upon the corroded underside of the car.

He'd hoped that meeting with that private investigator might've changed things. And yet, it didn't look that way.

Lorenzo felt impatient.

Oliver Rainsford was a powerful man. Why would anyone have taken Lorenzo's side against his? It was hardly equal when it came to each other's side of the story. The cards had always been stacked against him.

Lorenzo had little faith in the system.

He would give Stanley Messina one last chance.

But if that failed, maybe the only way to get justice for Ashleigh was to take matters into his own hands.

CHAPTER 20

As they walked away from the house, Stanley heard the front door close firmly behind them. Jack muttered under his breath, 'Not sure that went very well...'

'I only left you with her for five minutes,' said Stanley.

'Yeah, well she was pressing my buttons.'

From upstairs, Stanley had heard their raised voices. He and Bernadette had exchanged glances at the disturbance.

'What were you arguing about?'

They'd moved out of sight from the windows of the house. Stanley had drawn them to a halt on the pavement.

'She was trying to blame me for this mess not being sorted. Accused me of raking things up. She got under my skin. So I threw mud back at her.'

It wasn't professional. Surely Jack hadn't behaved like this when he'd been in the force?

'What do you mean? What 'mud' did you throw at her?'

'Oh, it was what we'd discussed. I asked a few questions. Didn't take me very long to find out that our hunch had been right. Oliver *was* engaged to another woman in the past. And he did leave her for Jacinta. I simply pointed out to her that perhaps she might like to reflect on the implications of that. Those in glass houses and all that...'

'It didn't sound as if she'd reacted very kindly to that.'

'Like a red rag to a bull. I asked her whether she'd been afraid of being traded in for a younger model. Said that Oliver had form. Pointed out that she had a lot to lose.'

Stanley liked to be in control of things. He preferred to follow an investigation in a neat and logical manner. There seemed little to be gained, however, from chastising his impulsive sidekick. Jack's outburst demonstrated an escalation in how he felt about the situation. He was certainly heavily invested.

'From Bernadette's account,' said Stanley, 'it was just about here that somebody shoved her to the ground.'

The pair of them looked solemnly at the raggedy bricks of the pavement.

'Do you think someone could've been hiding in one of the front gardens? Lying in wait for her?' asked Jack. 'Or did someone follow her, unnoticed?'

Stanley didn't answer. He mulled over the circumstances as he scanned the quiet suburban vista. He paid particular attention to where she'd fallen. He looked at where the pavement met the gutter.

An assailant.

Ashleigh.

His mind attempted to leap across potential explanations.

'Jacinta said we hadn't looked closely enough at Lorenzo Conti,' said Jack. 'She asked whether you knew he'd been hanging around…'

With a working theory now in mind, Stanley was unsurprised to hear this. It was all beginning to make sense.

The noise of an approaching vehicle brought both of them back starkly into the moment. It was a particularly outdated hatchback rumbling in what sounded like too low a gear. Stanley and Jack gawped as it drew to a halt beside them, the handbrake being pulled on with a vigorous crunch.

From the driver's door frantically emerged a red-faced woman.

'Are you the police?' she said, loudly. She blinked ferociously. Before they'd had a chance to answer she was reaching back into the car for her bag. 'You look like the police. Don't they say you can smell a copper?'

'I'm Stanley Messina, private investigator,' said Stanley. 'And this is former Detective Inspector Jack Sheppard.'

She pulled herself upright and peered at them through

frazzled eyeballs. 'We have to trust the authorities, don't we?' she said, her voice raised again in a peculiar erratic tone. Stanley sensed a woman on the edge.

'And you are?' asked Jack.

'I'm Magda. Bernadette's mother.' She brushed something unseen from her crumpled clothing before holding out her trembling hand. As they shook it, her manic face veered between an odd smile and being on the verge of tears. 'Has she been terribly hurt?'

'She's doing okay,' Stanley reassured her. 'She has a cut on her forehead but that will heal.'

'That might heal,' she echoed, 'but what about the *mental* scars. That's what makes me anxious. I worry about what it's done to her.'

Stanley nodded. 'Bernadette seems resilient.'

Her mother blinked again. She almost appeared to gulp the air around her. She twitched as if malfunctioning. 'How can such awful things *not* have changed her? Such violent and nasty things. Horrible things that should never happen to anyone. She used to have Ashleigh to confide in. Never wanted to talk about things with me. Daughters don't want to talk to their mothers, do they? But who does she have to share her thoughts with now?'

Once again her demeanour flashed between jovial and weepy.

'We're doing our very best to find out what's gone on,' said Jack.

She scooped her fingers through her hair leaving it standing on end more than before. 'You're still looking for a killer? He's still on the loose, isn't he?'

'Do you have any reason to suspect anyone of wanting to harm Bernadette?' asked Stanley.

Her face contorted, obviously affronted at the suggestion that anybody could take against her daughter. 'It's her being around these types of people. Look at it. What sense of reality do you have living in a house like that? They don't live normal lives. They're not like the rest of us.' Her eyes had grown wide.

She set off in a frumpy angry march towards the Rainsfords home.

'Not much like her daughter,' observed Jack.

'Hmmm.'

'Unhinged, would you say? Or just highly strung?'

Stanley wouldn't be drawn on a position. He was looking again at the pavement and gutter. Unless he was very much mistaken, things were beginning to make sense.

'There's nothing more to be achieved here now,' he said. 'I'll drop you back at home…'

Not more than an hour later, Stanley strode back through the town centre streets to his meagre lodgings. He hoped that Sylvia might not be in residence, instead out visiting the local *Wetherspoons*. The drinks were cheaper there, he reasoned, and the brisk trade probably allowed her to have double measures without judgement.

Even if she were to be around, she'd be ensconced in front of daytime television. She particularly enjoyed programmes about ex-pats living abroad. The voyeuristic pursuit of those in sunnier climes obviously provided an escape from the ratty view of Clifton Sands's backstreets through her net curtains. With her glued to the screen, he'd be able to slip into his room and close the door, take an opportunity alone to consider a picture that was revealing itself with increasing clarity.

As he passed the untidy small front gardens of neighbouring properties – many littered with discarded furniture, mattresses, and general junk – he too was struck by the sense of a shadow on his shoulder. It wasn't unusual to have to keep your wits about you. The crime rates here had soared beyond the averages in London and Brighton. There were often signs of the addiction problems that plagued the town.

Stanley told himself that he was being paranoid whilst simultaneously taking longer and faster steps to his destination.

At the front of the building, he fumbled with the latch on the wrought iron gate.

'Stanley?'

Stanley caught his breath and turned to see who had spoken. On seeing who it was, he said: 'You followed me?'

Lorenzo Conti wore a tight black vest that displayed the sinuous muscles on his arms and chest. A gold necklace hung around his neck. This man, thought Stanley, had many guises. The mechanic. The waiter. The boxer. And here, in broad daylight, he stood in his civvies somehow as an amalgam of all those different versions.

'You live here?' he said, unbelieving.

'Yes.' Stanley didn't know how it might look to be seen talking with Lorenzo like this. Jack wouldn't have like it. 'You want to talk?'

'I want answers.'

It was what everybody wanted.

Stanley quickly assessed the situation. With nowhere obvious for the two of them to speak publicly beyond prying eyes, he felt obliged to invite him inside. 'You better come in...'

They entered the drab hallway where scores of pamphlets advertising everything from stairlifts to pizza delivery were shoved against the skirting board. Stanley could think of no small talk to make as Lorenzo followed him up the dimly lit stairs, his hulking presence somehow more pronounced in the confines of the stairwell. On reaching the door to the flat, Lorenzo towered over Stanley as he slipped the key in the lock.

The flat appeared to be empty.

'Sylvia?' Stanley called out, but there was no reply. He ushered Lorenzo down to the privacy of his room and closed the door behind them.

Lorenzo, suddenly appearing bigger in the confined space than he had ever looked before, appraised the bare room with disbelieving eyes. Stanley glimpsed a horror at the single bed with its threadbare bedspread. Their being together in Stanley's bedroom struck him as absurd. He saw the space for what it was: sad and lonesome.

'Is this where a private investigator lives?' Lorenzo asked.

'I haven't judged you, Lorenzo. All I ask is for the same in return.'

'That's what she said too.'

'What do you mean?' asked Stanley. Was 'she' who he thought she was?

'It's what Ashleigh said to me. Almost word for word. She said that she'd never judged me, you know for the type of things I'd done, being in trouble with the police and everything...'

'And she confided in you something that she'd done? Something that she thought she might be judged for?'

It was as Stanley had begun to suspect. The picture was becoming ever clearer.

If Stanley's digs gave Lorenzo any doubt to his professional credentials, he swept them aside to share the tale Ashleigh had regaled, one that he believed nobody else was aware of.

'Who doesn't have skeletons in their closet?' said Lorenzo, looking around again at the sorry room.

Stanley backtracked: 'You said you want answers?'

'Yes,' said Lorenzo. 'I want to know what you did with it? With what I gave you?'

Stanley comprehended and reached down into the bedside drawer in which he kept his closest possessions. The golden object sparkled as he lifted it out on its intricate chain.

'Ashleigh's locket,' said Stanley. 'The locket she was believed to be wearing on the day she was killed.'

'I told you,' Lorenzo whispered, 'I found it in the desk drawer at the garage. I don't know how it got there. Somebody must've planted it. Somebody who wanted to put me in the frame.'

Just then, there was a sound of Sylvia returning.

'Who's that?' said Lorenzo.

'It's my landlady.'

'An odd kind of set up you've got going on.' Catching

Stanley off-guard, he reached decisively out and swiped the locket from his grasp. 'I thought you might've been able to help me. Thought you were different from that other detective.'

'I can help you,' said Stanley. 'I just need more time.'

'Time?' he said in a louder voice. Stanley felt sure that Sylvia would hear them. 'I'm sick and tired of having to wait. I want action. I want something to happen, for somebody to do something. And if that's not going to be you, then it might as well be me.'

'But Lorenzo, please…'

Stanley was brushed aside as Lorenzo stormed from the room. Slipping out into the corridor in his wake, he watched as the door to the flat slammed close and Sylvia's imposing silhouette moved into view.

Later, Stanley lay on the lumpy bed and traced the cracks in the plaster of the ceiling. He couldn't shake the vision of Sylvia's face, looking somewhat triumphant at having caught a young man leaving his bedroom. They hadn't exchanged words. Not yet. But Stanley knew that they were coming. And how he might be able to explain away Lorenzo's presence, he wasn't sure of yet.

Not for the first time, he wondered whether change was coming. It had only been intended as a temporary stopgap. Time, perhaps, to consider fully the next step.

His phone, on the bedside table, began to ring.

'Stanley Messina.'

'Hello. Is that the private investigator?'

'Yes. Speaking.'

'My name's Gary Hillman.'

The caller paused as if his name should mean something to him, but Stanley couldn't recall its significance.

They continued: 'You visited my Nan's salon? Said that you wanted to know whether we still had CCTV footage?'

Stanley sat bolt upright. 'Yes, that's right.'

'Saturday twenty-seventh of August? The day that girl was

murdered?'

'Yes,' said Stanley.

'I have it. When would you like to come and view it?'

CHAPTER 21

Living up to Clifton Sands's reputation as having one of the highest ratios of fast-food outlets to residents in the entire country, Gary Hillman suggested they meet at *Wicked Wings*.

'We can meet anywhere really,' he'd said on the phone. 'I've got everything stored on my laptop.'

Stanley looked at the red and yellow signage above the glass-fronted entrance. A chicken's head looked to be laughing next to the shop's name. Looking down the street, Stanley saw a proliferation of charity shops, nail bars and more outlets resembling the one he stood outside of.

Gary worked at one of the *Tesco Express* stores dotted throughout the town centre. He wore a light coat over his branded blue T-shirt. On such a warm day, Stanley wondered whether this was to disguise where he was employed. He was short and stout with a wispy attempt at a beard. A baseball cap on his head cast a shadow over his eyes.

'Sorry I'm late,' he said on seeing Stanley. He was out of breath. 'We were short staffed this morning and one of the deliveries arrived late.'

Pushing the door open, they were greeted by the scent of fried food. Looking at the tables and chairs screwed to the floor and the stark tiles on the floor and walls, Stanley thought it would be too grand to describe the place as a restaurant. The staff – dressed in what appeared to be a parody of hospitality – greeted Gary warmly as an obvious regular. They already knew what his order would be: a box of 'fiery wings', a side of fries and a Coca Cola.

'Let me get these,' said Stanley, stepping forward to the

counter whilst peering at the unfathomable menu illuminated above them, opting simply for a lemonade.

'Nan thinks I'm a technological wizard,' said Gary, squeezing himself between a table and chair with his tray of food. 'She's more at home with an abacus.'

He heaved the laptop case he'd been carrying over his shoulder onto the table and unzipped it.

'Have you always looked after the CCTV footage at her salon?' asked Stanley.

'These sorts of systems are pretty cheap and easy to use if you know how. Not much different from the doorbell cameras that link to your phone. The system we use stores each twenty-four hours of footage in a separate file.'

'And has there ever been any need to access the footage before?'

Gary nodded but couldn't speak immediately having plunged a handful of chips into his mouth. He chewed and swallowed. 'Money went missing once. We were able to look back over the days when it had gone and identify a staff member with their hand in the till. Bit naïve of them to think that they weren't being recorded.'

'Nothing else?'

'No,' said Gary, washing his chips down with a slurp on his straw. 'Nan didn't mention to me about the police visiting after that girl's murder. I think it slipped her mind, to be fair. And there was never any follow-up. Lucky that you came and asked actually. I usually go through and delete files that are over a year old.'

Gary opened the laptop and powered it up. The screen buzzed into life.

Stanley watched as folders were located and opened.

'August twenty seventh?'

'Yes,' said Stanley.

'Bingo!'

The file was clicked and a media player opened with a grainy image displaying a timer in the corner showing just after midnight on the day that Ashleigh had died. The image hovered from the ceiling, looking down across the chairs and mirrors. Through the front window, the streetscape was lit in a phosphorous glow. Stanley was relieved to see that the entrance to *Criminal Records* was unintentionally but blessedly clear to see.

'Don't worry,' said Gary, 'we don't have to watch it in real-time. We can skip forward. What time did you want to see?'

Stanley couldn't be sure. He thought of what he'd learnt, of where the key players had said they'd been that day. He thought too of the estimated time of Ashleigh's murder. It was pure conjecture, but he suggested a time and Gary scrolled forward to it.

The tone of the image changed. It was now daylight. The shop had an afternoon client sat beneath an old-fashioned dryer holding a magazine. Pedestrians milled by the window. A fan, Stanley noticed, rotated lazily on its base. A hot summer's day, just as they'd all described. And testament to that, across the busy street, the door to *Criminal Records* was propped open.

Gary sucked on a chicken bone. 'Don't think it's going to win an Oscar.'

'Wait!' said Stanley.

'What? What is it?'

'Can you pause?'

Gary duly obliged.

Stanley squinted at the screen. He'd missed something.

'What are we looking at?' said Gary.

'Look. The door to the record shop over the road is now shut. Can we rewind to see when it closed?'

A quick rewind revealed a snarl up of traffic on the road, in which a large truck stopped outside *Criminal Records* obscuring the clear view of the camera. When it moved on, the door was no longer open.

Stanley's mind whirred. He looked at the date and time stamp on the recording. Enough time for Reece to have slipped away to the Rainsfords's house? How long would the door remain closed?

The seconds and minutes on the clock ticked over. Stanley watched and waited until an anticipated revelation appeared at the closed door…

Jack sat alone at his mother's dining room table. He didn't notice the bone china figurines in the glass cabinet looking sadly at his lonely presence. He'd grown blind to the flowers on the wallpaper and the pink carpet.

In the past, his dark thoughts had often only troubled him after consuming pints at the pub. Recently, however, they'd become more persistent. It was, of course, the very reason he'd contacted Stanley Messina in the first place. Not that he'd held an idea how things might improve. Just a hope, he supposed, that things might be different.

He stared at the blank piece of paper and pen.

Looking back, he wondered how life might've been different had he made other decisions or choices. How often, he thought, he spoke in the past tense. As if those opportunities were now gone.

What would life look like now if he'd never worried about what other people thought? Would he be happier if he'd lived the life he'd wanted to?

Jacinta had been right. He was pathetic.

Moving into his mother's bungalow had been the first step towards it, he supposed. Losing interest in his own possessions. Losing interest in everything, really…

How silly to have pinned the last throw of the dice in the hands of a virtual stranger. Totally unfair to have put that on Stanley.

He picked up the pen.

It's what you did, wasn't it. Write a letter?

At first, the words didn't sound like him at all. He re-read them as if written by a stranger.

It was, he realised, him saying goodbye.

*

It didn't cross Stanley's mind to inform Jack of what he'd learnt from Gary Hillman's CCTV footage. Stanley had been employed to investigate. And that is what he'd done.

Having thanked Gary for his assistance, Stanley traced a particular route on foot through the streets which led him ultimately to the doorstep of *Criminal Records*. The door, as it had been in the past, was open until Stanley entered and kicked away the wedge that propped it ajar.

Reece, at the counter, looked up as if to protest until he saw who it was that had entered.

There were no customers in the shop. Stanley flipped the sign on the door to 'Closed'.

Always strange, Stanley thought, to re-enact things that have come before. To put oneself in other people's shoes.

The music emanating from the speakers was trance-like. There was a low hypnotic beat. Stanley thought of the stylus upon the record, bringing back to life sounds from the past.

'Oh, it's you,' said Reece. If not mistaken, Stanley detected a tone of resignation. As if, perhaps, he'd always expected this moment to arrive.

'We need to talk.'

'I said before, I've told you everything I know…'

Stanley passed the well-ordered racks of vinyl covers. 'But you didn't.'

'I…'

A barely discernible flash of panic crossed Reece's face. It might've been missed by a casual observer. And yet, Stanley saw it with extraordinary clarity.

Reece turned and lifted the arm from the record. The music halted abruptly with a gentle thud and the shop was quiet apart from the muffled rumble of traffic outside.

'What I have to ask you is extremely serious,' said Stanley. 'I suggest you answer entirely honestly. Failure to do so may implicate you in a crime more serious than the one you have committed.'

Stanley watched the colour drain from Reece's face.

'Let's look at it like a story,' said Stanley. 'That's often the easiest way to make sense of these things. Always best to start at the beginning.

'Once upon a time there were two boys. One – Oliver Rainsford – came from a wealthy family. He wasn't academically gifted, but that didn't matter. His parents could afford to pay the exorbitant fees at *Manor House* school. That's the thing with money, isn't it? It helps open doors.

'The other boy – you, Reece James – was different. You were bright. But your family was poor. So it was through your academic ability that you were awarded a scholarship to study at the same school.

'Whilst coming from very different backgrounds, a striking and uncanny resemblance between these two boys brought them together. Their physical similarity led many to believe that they could have been twins. Their friendship was close, maybe even conspiratorial. What either of them lacked, they made up for via their doppelganger.

'Am I right?' asked Stanley.

Reece shrugged. 'You've condensed it a bit simplistically.'

'Yes,' said Stanley. 'For the sake of brevity, I have. We could discuss how you were both motivated by different things or how your family backgrounds influenced your outlooks. We could examine whether you were both as connected to the networks that *Manor House* promoted. That would be going round the houses though, wouldn't it?

'So let's skip forward in the story to that moment that every young person must face; the crossroads from school to whatever lies beyond.

'Despite the school's best efforts to convince you, the prospect of university and higher education didn't appeal to you. Too much of a free spirit, you thought.

'For Oliver though, the prized offer of a place at a top red brick university meant everything to him. It would elevate him in the eyes of his family and increase his chances of building an independent fortune. There was only one problem though, wasn't there?'

Reece chewed his bottom lip. 'It was Oliver's idea. He asked me. As a friend.'

'He asked you to sit the entrance exam for his university admission.'

'He was worried that he'd flunk it. So he gave me his ID and I sat the exam in his place.'

Stanley pictured the SILENCE – EXAM IN PROGRESS notice pinned to the closed door.

'It was done,' said Stanley. 'A simple deception. A lie that faded into the past as you and Oliver drifted apart, your schoolboy friendship not built on anything substantial enough to sustain it into adulthood.

'Only, perhaps, when Ashleigh told you that she was moving in to work as a nanny for a wealthy family named the Rainsfords did the deception return to you. A little research on your behalf, maybe, shocked you at the financial divide between you and Oliver. His business, reputation and fortune appeared to be built on the promotion of education and qualifications.

'You seized an opportunity and began to send him anonymous letters threatening to reveal the truth about what had happened. You wanted money in return for silence. Blackmail, pure and simple.'

Reece looked ashen. 'I pushed it too far. I was still grieving for Helen. I was living in a fog. I'd never have gone through with ruining Oliver's business.'

'But Oliver wasn't to know that.'

'No,' admitted Reece.

Stanley recalled the CCTV footage. Eventually the door to the shop had opened and Oliver had emerged from within. A deal had been struck. Reece's silence had been bought with a considerable lump sum payment. Oliver could never be sure that the begging bowl wouldn't return in the future, but for the moment crisis had been averted.

'Ok,' said Reece. 'We cheated. It's not as if anyone died...'

The note, written in untidy handwriting, was folded and poked beneath a windscreen wiper on Oliver's car. He thought of a bucket with holes appearing in it. Just when one seemed to be filled, another one sprung up unexpectedly.

He had dealt with such threats before. He would see this one off too.

Little did he know of the danger that lay ahead...

CHAPTER 22

At the end of the working day, an exodus of vehicles drove away from the industrial estate. The greasy spoon van at which queues of trades people would queue for bacon sandwiches and burgers closed its hatch. And the warehouse units pulled down their metal shutters leaving an eerie feeling of abandonment. With no reason for any visitors at night, the area became a ghost town.

Classic Auto Repairs was also now closed, its shutters too pulled down and the door to the customer reception locked. The radio that blared throughout the day had been switched off and the noisy tools were now laid down and silent.

Lorenzo paced the dirty concrete floor, trying to ignore the muffled sounds coming from metres away. He'd turned most of the lights off, careful not to attract any attention. Unlikely though, seeing as how deserted the area became of an evening.

He still wore his overalls, oil-stained from a day's work.

He looked at the pit. This place was full of dangers. How easy it would be to have an accident here.

The rage, which he'd spent so long trying to suppress, began to boil in his bones. It made him want to lash out, to punch something. His hands curled into fists.

He looked at the clock on the wall. Would he come? He'd said he would.

'Come alone,' Lorenzo had insisted. 'Don't bring anyone with you.'

But would he follow his instruction? He'd never struck him as a man to do as he was told.

He reached into his pocket and from it he pulled the golden

locket that Ashleigh had always worn around her neck. How had it come to be in a drawer of the desk here at the garage? It looked brighter than ever against his grimy fingers. He felt its cool exterior against his skin, trying to bring back the feeling of Ashleigh as if her departed spirit might still linger within. Silently, almost deferentially, he opened the locket on its miniscule hinges. There, as he'd looked at countless times, were two faces: Ashleigh's mother, Helen. And his own.

What other proof did he need that they'd been the two most important people to her. She had literally held them close to her heart, always.

They'd spoken so much about their future and the dreams they shared beyond the limits of a rundown seaside town. He thought again of how Ashleigh had made him want to be a better man. Being with her had made his petty criminal ways look childish. With her, he wanted to take on the responsibility of being an adult. To forge a path away from what others – and he was thinking of his family here – thought that he should be.

He closed the locket and put it back in his pocket.

He was getting impatient. Surely he should be here by now? Where was he?

Another muffled grunt sounded from the shadows. If they were words being said, Lorenzo couldn't hear them.

All in good time.

A knock sounded on the metal door.

Lorenzo steadied himself. He had waited long enough. He'd been patient.

He noticed, surprised, the spiders that lived in the rafters of the warehouse. Funny how he'd never seen them before. Their webs hung in intricate white swathes.

On opening the door, Lorenzo was confronted by the hound dog expression of the detective who'd so often pointed the finger of suspicion at him. The man looked different now, worn down and aged by the whole experience. It had taken its toll on them all.

'You're alone?'

'Yes,' said Jack as he stepped across the threshold.

Lorenzo bolted and locked the door. This would end how he decided now.

'You're ready to talk?' asked Jack. 'You said that you were ready for me to hear your confession.'

It was the truth, of sorts. Although, of course, Lorenzo had drawn him here under false pretences. On the phone, Jack Sheppard had sounded distant as if his thoughts were occupied with other things. But he had taken the bait.

'Almost,' said Lorenzo, speaking over the muffled groans behind him. He stepped in their direction. 'I want you to hear *a* confession. Not *my* confession.'

The look on Jack's face was a picture as his eyes adjusted to the dimly lit interior and came to see a figure tied to a chair with a sack over their head. They wriggled and squirmed against the rope that bound them tight. Lorenzo couldn't deny that it felt good to be calling the shots at last. Not to feel endlessly at the mercy of other people's incompetence at finding Ashleigh's killer.

'What the...?' said Jack.

Like some perverse magic trick, Lorenzo ripped off the sack with a one-handed flourish. Beneath, his captive was red-faced and revealed to have had a gag tied around his mouth.

'Oliver?' asked Jack.

His eyes pleaded with Jack to be set free. He tried to say something, but his frustrated words were caught in the material over his mouth. It was hard to believe that the proud – arrogant, even – man that Jack knew could be the same as this restrained sorry-looking creature.

'You were so caught up with your own assumptions about me,' Lorenzo began, 'that you couldn't bring yourself to believe that someone as successful as Oliver Rainsford could be guilty of such a crime. You both, in a way, had *power*. And powerful men stick together, don't they? They protect one another. Well, today you will hear it from the horse's mouth. And you will listen...'

From the workbench, Lorenzo had chosen the heaviest wrench available. Oliver's eyes widened in terror as the implement was grasped and raised into the air. It was a suitable weapon, capable of inflicting damage and pain. A certain way, surely, of making him speak.

'This isn't the way to go about things,' said Jack who had raised both his hands in a sad looking gesture to placate him.

'Don't come any closer.' Lorenzo untied the gag from Oliver's mouth who gasped for air.

'He's crazy!' wheezed Oliver. 'He lured me here. Told me he knew things about me that I wouldn't want shared.'

'I do,' said Lorenzo. 'But I want to hear these things from *you*. I want you to say these things aloud in front of the detective.'

Oliver shook his head. 'Whatever you think you know isn't true. Just untie me. We can talk about this like adults.'

This was rich coming from him, thought Lorenzo. He hadn't treated Ashleigh like an adult. There had definitely been a power imbalance. A position of authority that Lorenzo believed Oliver had exploited.

'Ashleigh didn't know what she was getting into,' said Lorenzo. 'After her mum died, she didn't know which direction to take. She'd only just left school. She didn't know who she was after having been a carer for so long. Being a live-in nanny seemed like an obvious way forward.

'But she didn't realise what she was getting herself into. Your family life wasn't caring, as her own had been. Your home is like a fortress. It's a place that you can control. You use money to lure people in and then manipulate them.'

Oliver let out a frustrated exhale of breath. 'What's the point of this? You're just rambling, grasping at straws. It sounds like you were jealous that Ashleigh was living a life you could *never* provide for her. Is it that you know that you'd never be good enough for her?'

Lorenzo swung the wrench and caught it on a box of car parts on the bench which duly crashed to the floor and scattered on the concrete. He pointed the trembling weapon into Oliver's face. 'You take that back,' he spat.

'I won't,' said Oliver. 'The fact you're threatening me with violence shows what type of low life you are. A no hoper.'

'Okay, let's just take it easy,' Jack spoke up. 'There's no need for this to get out of hand.'

The air thrummed with tension and heavy breathing from the sparring duo.

'What is it you think you know about me?' Oliver asked Lorenzo.

'Ashleigh wasn't sure what type of relationship you and Jacinta had. She said that behind closed doors you often argued. The perfect image you portrayed to the world wasn't the reality. She told me she thought you had a roving eye. I should have put two and two together then.'

Oliver shook his head again. 'Ashleigh was young. She was naïve. Her outlook on the world was optimistic, despite the difficult things that had happened in her life, losing both her parents. That's what we all loved about her, didn't we?'

'Love?' said Lorenzo. '*Love?*'

'Just because we were her employer, didn't mean that we weren't fond of her.'

'Exactly that.'

'What do you mean?'

'You *were* fond of her, weren't you? Too fond of her.'

Lorenzo looked for a reaction from his captive.

'What? No!'

'You overstepped the boundaries. You'd been drinking...'

Oliver's demeanour changed. 'That was a misunderstanding.'

'Not on Ashleigh's behalf,' said Lorenzo.

'It was something and nothing. Ashleigh understood that.'

'Something and nothing? That you forced yourself upon her? Do you call that something and nothing?'

Oliver struggled against the restraints tying him to the chair.

'Is this true?' asked Jack.

'No,' said Oliver. 'I swear to you that wasn't what happened.

I made a foolish drunken pass at her. I'd read the signs wrong. But she said no, and I respected that. I swear on my daughter's life that that's what happened.'

'Liar,' said Lorenzo. 'You forced yourself on her. And she was carrying your child.'

'You're mad!' said Oliver. 'This is all absolute fantasy.'

The red mist grew in Lorenzo's sight. It was hard to separate the now and then. He thought of all the dreams they'd shared together, all the opportunities that lay ahead of them. To have them all snatched away by this disgusting letch of a human being. What was there to live for now? Nothing would ever replace what he'd had with Ashleigh.

'Why won't you tell us this is what happened?' shouted Lorenzo. 'Tell us!'

'Because it's not true…'

'Perhaps a little persuasion will loosen your tongue?'

Lorenzo picked up a plastic can from the corner. It was heavy. He unscrewed the lid and the strong scent of petrol made his nostrils twitch.

With vigorous splashing arcs he proceeded to empty the contents of the can over Oliver and his surroundings.

'You've got to stop him!' Oliver called to Jack.

With that, Jack leapt forward and attempted to grab the can from Lorenzo's grasp. They tussled over it as the final drops covered them both. They gripped one another by their collars, panting.

Just then, Jack's phone began to ring in his pocket. Distracted for only a moment, he didn't see Lorenzo's fist approaching. Too slow to react and avoid the blow. He staggered back from the impact, clattering against the garage paraphernalia. Before he knew it, Lorenzo's hand was rummaging in his pocket and had claimed Jack's mobile.

'It's your pal, Stanley Messina,' said Lorenzo, looking at the caller display. He dropped the phone to the ground and stamped his heel onto it, shattering it with a vicious crunch.

'What I want to know,' Oliver suddenly piped up, 'is why

wait until now?'

'Yes,' said Jack, nursing where he'd been punched. 'That's what I was wondering.'

Oliver continued: 'If Ashleigh told you this is what happened – which, I might add, it *didn't* – why didn't you share this information with the police? Why keep it to yourself?'

Lorenzo wished she had told him. If she had, he might've been able to do something. The outcome might've been completely different.

'Ashleigh?' he said. 'It wasn't *Ashleigh* who told me.'

'Then who?' asked Jack. '*Who* told you this is what happened?'

The heady liquid dripped in puddles on the floor. What did it matter who had told him?

It would be painful. But it would soon be over.

This is where it would end...

CHAPTER 23

Forty-five minutes earlier, on the other side of town, Stanley had a sense of things coming full circle as he parked his car outside the Rainsford's house. As he stepped out on to the road, he noticed that the air was a little cooler and the sun slightly lower in the sky. The oncoming change of season, however, was far from his mind. His thoughts, instead, were focused on what had to be done.

The walk to the front door was familiar, and yet it felt different seeing everything through new eyes. It was the same place and yet somehow entirely transformed when viewed via the prism of all the facts. The truth has a way of doing that, thought Stanley. Shedding new light on places and people. Revealing them to be something other than what they portray.

It was Jacinta who answered the door this time.

'You again,' she said.

'May we speak?' asked Stanley.

At first she looked reluctant and he wondered whether she'd allow him in. But then, with a sigh, she relented.

They walked through the grand hallway and into the vast kitchen with its glass doors. On the terraced garden, Stanley saw the little girl playing with her nanny. Theirs was a special little bond.

Jacinta looked tired. Her face was gaunt and strained. She pulled up a chair at the table and slumped wearily upon it.

'Do you think I'm harsh?' she said.

'I think this must've taken a toll on you,' Stanley replied.

'I just want it all to go away. It's been like a curse. I think people imagine that our life is comfortable – luxurious even.

They don't see that the trappings of wealth don't mean anything if you're constantly reminded of something terrible that happened.'

Stanley wouldn't judge. He'd come here to listen.

'That is all well and good,' he said, 'but you *were* afraid of losing the comfortable life. Am I right?'

She sat silently.

Stanley continued: 'You came to learn that Oliver was being blackmailed.'

'I wasn't snooping,' she said. 'I've never been that type of person. I just found one of the envelopes by chance. It sort of shook me. To think that Oliver might have secrets or that he might not have been being completely honest with me.'

'I understand.'

'You do?'

'Of course,' said Stanley. 'The lives we live are so often an illusion. They're built upon fragile foundations. What we see on the surface is rarely the whole story.'

She chewed one of her manicured nails. He saw a softer side. A side that she liked to keep hidden.

'It changed my perspective, I suppose,' she said, quietly.

'Did it make you wonder whether he might lie to you about other things too?'

She looked to be considering her answer carefully, as if unsure of betraying her husband. 'I had been the *other* woman once. Not too far a stretch of the imagination to think that he might be possible of it again. What do they say about history repeating itself?'

Stanley had already guessed this was the case. Although, he knew more sides of the story than perhaps she was aware. He thought back to the day of the murder on which Oliver had met with Reece in his shop to confront him.

'The day Ashleigh was murdered,' said Stanley, 'you were on the beach.'

'Yes. We were there as a family.'

'He said he had business to attend to. He slipped away. Did

you think he was going to see Ashleigh?'

Her eyes, of which he'd once seen as cold, now looked scared. To admit this, not only meant that she was admitting to herself that he might be capable of cheating, but also that he might've been guilty of killing Ashleigh. She had stood by him as a watertight alibi.

She didn't know, as Stanley did, that Oliver hadn't been at the house. It couldn't have been him.

'I think Ashleigh had turned his head. She'd caught his roving eye.'

Again, Stanley wouldn't judge.

'It must've been a terrible shock to have found Ashleigh's body,' said Stanley.

She trembled. 'I'd never seen anyone dead before. But there was no doubt about it.'

'You acted instinctively, would you say, in the moment?'

'I...'

'Yes?'

'It was a survival instinct, I suppose.'

'You removed Ashleigh's locket from her.'

It was a statement, not a question.

'I thought it might be a way of making sure that he'd never leave me. An insurance policy, if you like.'

Stanley thought that she might be thinking as much of her financial security as her marriage.

'So if the spotlight shone too closely on Oliver, you could use the locket to place the blame somewhere else?'

She hung her head.

Stanley knew that it was she who had slipped the locket into the desk drawer at the garage. A simple way to implicate Lorenzo for a crime that he hadn't committed. It said something of her that she might condemn an innocent man. It tested Stanley's empathy for her.

A shriek of laughter pierced their solemn discussion. Sophie was rolling on the grass as Bernadette tickled her.

'Sometimes it hardly feels real,' said Jacinta. 'It's like some terrible story. Something you might read in a book...'

It was as if she'd read his mind.

'When you found Ashleigh, she'd been reading a novel.'

'Yes,' she replied.

'Can you remember the title of the book?'

'Oh yes,' said Jacinta. 'In fact, the police returned it to us. I don't know why, but I put it back on the shelf. Would you like to see?'

'Yes. Yes, please.'

As he stepped out into the garden, Stanley sensed a going over of the plants. The foliage, once lush and vibrant, had faded into russet tones.

The little girl, still rolling merrily on one of the terraced lawns, didn't see him at first.

'Sophie,' he called, 'Mummy's looking for you inside.'

Her flushed face swivelled to see who had spoken. She scrambled to her feet, abandoning any game that was being played. The draw of her mother a strong one.

As she passed Stanley, she said, 'You were here before. With your friend.'

'You have a good memory.'

'I do,' she said proudly as she marched inside.

Time stood still for a moment as Stanley walked up the wide steps. There was no breeze and the leaves and blades of grass stood motionless.

'We like to think we're important to them,' said Bernadette as he ascended towards her. 'But all they really want is to be with their parents.'

'Not easy accepting we're not as wanted as we'd hoped.'

He'd reached the level on which the decrepit summerhouse sat. Symbolic, perhaps, that they should meet at the very place where Ashleigh had been found.

She took a sharp intake of breath as he reached out to the handle on the door. It squeaked as he turned it but gave way surprisingly easily. He paused momentarily out of some kind of respect for the young woman who had been found there. Then he pushed further and the musty scent of somewhere that hadn't been touched wafted towards him.

Grasping the handle, he looked at her. She still wore the plaster on her forehead.

'On that afternoon, Ashleigh was sitting in here,' said Stanley. 'She was reading a book, one that she'd randomly selected from Jacinta's bookshelf. The house was empty as Sophie was with her parents at the beach. She was entirely alone both physically and with her thoughts. Until a visitor arrived through the gate at the end of the garden. A gate which there had never been reason to keep locked before.'

Bernadette's eyes flickered.

Stanley wondered if she was remembering how it had been. He asked directly: 'You came to confront her?'

She looked to be considering whether to speak or not, but with a brief shrug she said, 'I'd overheard them talking.'

'Ashleigh and Lorenzo,' stated Stanley, already having joined the dots up.

'You'll think I was being nosey. And I suppose I was. But Ashleigh was my best friend. My *only* friend. I cared for her and wanted to make sure that the boy she'd fallen for was for real.'

It was truth, of a sort. It had crossed Stanley's mind that she might've ear-wigged in the hope of finding reason to doubt the companion who was stealing away her one true friend.

Stanley recalled Lorenzo's account of the story Ashleigh had told. Today, however, he wanted to hear it from her.

As Bernadette's hands began to shake, Stanley was reminded of the brief interaction with her mother. 'Go on…' he said.

'Ashleigh said that at school there had been a girl nobody liked. She was known for being a compulsive liar. Always making up exaggerated stories that everybody knew weren't true. The girl had been a target for bullies. Targeting her had become almost something of a sport amongst the other students.

'At first, I was confused. I couldn't think who she was talking about. Until…'

'Until?'

'She told Lorenzo that she'd done something bad. She didn't know why. She'd been young and thought that it might endear her to those who ruled the roost on the playground.'

'What did she do?'

'She lured the unpopular girl to a cupboard. It was a prank, you see. She tricked her into thinking that a boy would be there. It was the cupboard in which the Science department kept all the chemicals and hearts and eyes for dissection. All the things the bullied girl hated the most. On locking her inside, Ashleigh went gleefully to tell her peers what she'd done, hoping to share the joke. But almost immediately the guilt had consumed her. Before she had the chance to tell anyone else she was running back to the cupboard where the frantic screams and banging of the trapped girl within sounded.

'The girl was having a panic attack. She was so relieved and grateful that Ashleigh had heard her and rescued her. She had no idea that the person who'd locked her in and the person who'd released her were one and the same person.'

Stanley wondered what it meant that she spoke in the third person. Some kind of distancing there? A schism between her body and her mind?

As if seeing incomprehension in Stanley's expression, she continued: 'It wasn't the prank. Well, not entirely. It was the years of her making me believe that we were actually friends. When all the time she was just trying to make herself feel better for what she'd done. Trying to convince herself that she wasn't the type of person who'd been capable of doing such a thing.'

'You asked her directly, right here, if your friendship was real?'

'She said she needed time to focus on herself, what with her mum dying and everything. Said that she couldn't listen to my stories anymore.'

Stanley didn't think it sounded unreasonable. But clearly Bernadette had construed it otherwise. She had taken it as a rejection. She had heard what she'd chosen to hear.

'She turned away from you for an instant,' said Stanley. 'Maybe to pick up her book? And in that moment…'

'I wasn't thinking,' said Bernadette. 'I saw a child's cricket bat lying on the floor. The next thing I knew, she was lying on the floor. She wasn't breathing.'

How easy, Stanley thought, to have concealed the murder weapon afterwards amongst other toys at the nursery.

The way in which Bernadette had viewed Ashleigh had changed everything. All a matter of perspective. Just as in this case, Stanley thought. The stories that had been spun had skewed their way of seeing. The power of telling tales. There was the story as to how Ashleigh had confessed about fearing she was pregnant. And the one about Oliver being drunk and forcing himself upon her. Not to mention the fabricated tale of having been assaulted. Easy to cut oneself with a knife and throw it away down a convenient drain.

He'd almost forgotten the object in his hand. It was a small book. The pages were yellow and well-worn. He held it aloft, it's title blazing: *'Between Now And Forever.'*

'It's what you said to me,' said Stanley. 'The exact words. It's how I knew you'd been here at the time of the murder.'

'Oh, a love story!' she laughed. 'And to think, if she hadn't met Lorenzo…' An admission that she wouldn't have cared that her supposed friendship with Ashleigh would've continued under a lie. 'What a tragedy if he should take things into his own hands now.'

'What do you mean?'

'They'll be together now. Lorenzo, Oliver and that failed detective friend of yours…'

Stanley pulled out his mobile. Her crazy lies had misled them all.

Jack wasn't answering.

What it meant that he felt an overwhelming sense of concern

for Jack Sheppard, he didn't know. A surge of emotion flooded him.

He grabbed her shoulders. 'Where the bloody hell are they?' he said. 'Tell me!'

CHAPTER 24

The wheels of Stanley's car screeched to a halt outside *Classic Auto Repairs*. He leapt from the vehicle, hoping that he wasn't too late to prevent a catastrophe.

'Lorenzo!' he shouted, banging his fists against the metal doors of the garage. 'Lorenzo, let me in! You've got it all wrong…'

At first, he feared he was too late. The industrial unit emanated a crashing air of defeat.

'Lorenzo!' he called again. 'Open up!'

But then, there came the sound of a lock being turned and, with an overwhelming smell of petrol fumes, Lorenzo's quizzical face emerged from within.

'Wrong?' he asked.

Beyond his outline, in the gloom, Stanley clocked Jack slumped on the floor and what looked like Oliver tied to a chair. Neither appeared to be moving.

'It was Bernadette,' said Stanley. 'Bernadette killed Ashleigh. She's confessed to it all.'

Now wasn't the time to be expanding on all the details.

'But she told me…' Lorenzo started, before his shoulders slumped in a dawning realisation. He looked deflated, broken by Bernadette's convincing tales. She had drawn them all into her unhappy web.

'Stanley?' a familiar voice croaked.

'Jack?' Stanley pushed his way past Lorenzo, who appeared to have been frozen, lost in trying to make sense of it all.

'Are you okay?' asked Stanley, rushing to him and crouching down at his crumpled frame. He was sodden in glistening liquid. A bruise looked to be forming around his eye.

'No broken bones,' said Jack.

Stanley found his hand resting on the man's knee in relief. Their eyes met, only to be interrupted by a slow tortured groan. It sounded like a wounded animal.

'What's going on?'

'It's okay, Oliver,' said Stanley, moving quickly to attend to him. 'It's all over. Everything's okay...'

Later, as the swirl of events began to settle, Stanley insisted that Jack leave his car at the garage and let Stanley drive him back across town. And for once, Jack didn't argue. His brush with disaster had left him in something of a sanguine state. Knowing Jack, Stanley thought, it wouldn't last for long. Wasn't he made of strong stuff?

The car journey offered them an opportunity to share one another's version of events. Neither of them wanting, perhaps, to admit that they'd kept each other in the dark, not having shared everything they'd learnt.

'Bernadette, eh?' said Jack. 'To think she'd been under our noses all this time.'

'She was a convincing storyteller.'

'And actress.'

'Yes,' said Stanley. 'I suppose she was.'

'Quick to confess too?'

This had also struck Stanley. 'Sometimes people want to unburden themselves. They're just waiting for an opportunity to do it.'

'Makes you think, doesn't it?'

After what had just happened, Stanley saw that this was a window of time in which both were prepared to let their guard down. They were in reflective mood. He'd go as far as saying philosophical.

Jack continued: 'Makes you wonder whether we've got this whole business of life wrong. As if it's all back to front somehow.'

'In what way?'

'Well, take Oliver's business for example...'

'*Progressive Pathways?*'

'Yes,' said Jack. 'He's made a fortune teaching people how to present themselves in different ways just to climb a slippery pole. Helping them to be something else in order to open doors which would otherwise remain closed to them.'

Stanley wasn't sure it was quite as simple as that, but he took Jack's point.

'Do you think we can choose who we want to be in life?' asked Stanley.

'I'd like to think so,' Jack replied. 'But maybe life has other ideas. You only have to look at this whole sorry business with Ashleigh James to see that. Her death was one thing. And then how it's changed all the people around her ever since is another thing altogether.'

Stanley concentrated on his driving but noticed Jack turn his gaze on the passing panorama of life: pedestrians, net curtains, front gardens. For once he didn't appear to be looking for trouble.

'Ashleigh's death,' said Jack, 'makes you realise that none of us know how long we have. So we might as well make the most of it...'

Stanley wasn't sure whether this observation was for his benefit or Jack's. It could be applied to both of them.

It might've been in Stanley's imagination that Jack moved slowly from the car at their destination - slower than simply accounting for his injuries – had it not been for Jack saying, 'I suppose it's the end to us working together then.'

'Let's get you inside,' Stanley said, side-stepping the conversation. They slammed the car doors shut, leaving perhaps their unguarded philosophical selves within.

Jack's bedraggled appearance looked at odds with the familiar trappings of suburbia.

Stanley followed up the garden path. He looked at Jack's

broad shoulders as a key was inserted into the frosted glass front door.

'You can't turn down the offer of a proper drink now,' said Jack hopefully. 'Not on work hours anymore.'

Stanley saw little reason to put up a fight. 'You ought to clean yourself up.'

Jack grinned. 'I'll go and have a shower. The beers are in the fridge. You can be mother.'

The kitchen was something of a time warp. A soft light filtered through the window, making the old lino and dated units shine almost nostalgically. Even the tiles were decorated with genteel pastoral scenes.

A humming old-fashioned free-standing fridge freezer revealed itself to glow inside with few fresh vegetables. True to his word, however, Jack had stashed it optimistically with Italian lager as well as his own various ales.

Jack would drink his from the bottle no doubt, but Stanley set about searching the cabinets for a glass for himself. A bottle opener was located in one of the drawers. He popped open his bottle and looked for a bin to put the redundant top.

There, underneath the sink, a plastic swing-top was full to the brim with rubbish. He reached out to dispose of the bottle top only to catch sight of a crumpled sheet of paper protruding from within.

He peered at it inquisitively. His fingers stretched out the creases.

He shouldn't have. It was intruding. But he began to read…

Dear Mum

I don't think I've ever written you a letter before. So this is a bit of a first! And I realise that I've left it too late. Which means I'm writing this as much for me as it might've been for you. I should've done this years ago but there never seemed to be a right time. But recently, events have made me want to share something I have hidden from the world for a long time.

You've always supported and encouraged me. I love you as I know you love me too. I've struggled with thinking that my truth wouldn't align with your faith and expectations. I worried that a life I might lead would disappoint you. This is why I've hesitated in sharing this aspect of my life with you.

I thought it would be easier to write than say aloud – although that isn't proving to be the case. I am gay. There, it's done. Three words that have tortured me for decades. It does not change who I am to you. I am still the same person. I expect you might be afraid that telling others this would put me at risk. You'd probably be disappointed that an idea of how my life might look might never happen. You'd be worried I'd be lonely or isolated. Well, the truth is I am lonely. And I'm tired of living a lie. I probably don't fit your idea of what 'gay' might look like. But I've come to see that there isn't a 'one size fits all'. It's just a part of who I am.

I want to live a fulfilling life, while time is still on my side. And I'd like to think that in time you would've come to accept – celebrate even – the person I hope to become. I want to be authentic. I want to shape my future in a way that feels right and true for me. This doesn't take away our memories or times we've shared together.

Who would believe that a middle-aged son could be so scared? I'm terrified to be honest. But I need to do this for my own peace of mind. As I said, with hindsight I should've done it years ago…

I will always love you and be here for you.

Forever
Jack

*

Stanley woke early the next morning with the optimism of a

new beginning. It was something that had been an alien feeling to him for many years. He dressed and tip-toed about, doing his best not to raise Slyvia from her hungover slumber. Her early-morning wrath was preferably avoided.

With his renewed sense of purpose, he opened the drawer to his bedside table once more. There within, embodying so much more than its meagre form, was a key with a plastic numbered fob attached to it. He reached out and pocketed it before slipping on his coat. The mornings were becoming cooler. Autumn proper would arrive shortly.

He could've driven but opted instead to head there on foot, shutting the front door and setting off at a brisk pace. Early morning Clifton Sands was a ratty place, as if it hadn't yet put on its fancy clothes for the day. It was endearing in a rundown kind of way. A privilege, almost, to be a part of its fabric rather than just a tourist.

Who could blame him for wanting to protect himself? There'd been so much to cope with. It had been overwhelming. Much easier in the moment to – quite literally – box everything of his old life up and label it as something to be dealt with in the future. There were things in there that would hurt him. It would be painful. It would take strength.

But he thought of Jack.

If one demon could be conquered, couldn't others?

The place at that time in the morning was deserted. Why anybody should need access to it twenty-four seven, Stanley couldn't fathom.

Lock 'Em Up Self Storage! the signage above the door proclaimed. Stanley felt almost removed from his own body. He felt as if he was about to reunite with someone from his past. That person being himself.

The fob opened the main front door with a beep. He hadn't been here since the day the removal van had brought everything. Only the monthly debit on his bank statement confirmed that the contents were still secure.

A sign with numbers and arrows reminded him of where his

cage was located.

He walked alone.

The echoing corridor brought back to him the horror of being inside: the shouting of men's voices, the clanging of keys, the slamming of cell doors.

He reached the spot in the company of the word that had haunted his recent investigation…

Vulnerable.

The time had come. It was a risk. But wasn't everything in life?

With a deep breath, Stanley slid the key into the lock and turned it.

Change lay within.

And now the door was open…

THE END

NOTE FROM THE AUTHOR

I hope you enjoyed reading Death Behind Closed Doors as much as I enjoyed writing it.

Reviews are critical to the success of an author's career and I'd be very grateful if you could write one on Amazon. Just follow the Amazon sales page where you purchased the title to leave your review and rating.

To keep up to date with my new releases please follow me online at **www.twitter.com/jon_neal_author** and **www.facebook.com/JonNealAuthor**

Thank you for taking the time to read my work.

JN

Printed in Great Britain
by Amazon